Anathea

By,

J.R. Packard

Chapters

CHAPTER 1

Creating a God

Sheep follow, and that has always been a longtime fact of life. Innocent at first, easily susceptible to instinctual animalistic tendencies following their childish purity, always to remain ignorant of wisdom, intellectual sense, and morality. The human, however–he who tends their movements across the pastures–knows himself, the differentiation between right and wrong, and grows as time passes ever on. Knowledge: it is the fine line that separates humans from beasts. Such natural order no longer existed in the *New World.* The most ferocious, unforgiving bear that acts on no more than pure mindlessness would shutter at the sight of what a person had descended into in the late 2060s.

The past was filled with fools and devilish people, according to the "most venerable" global dictator that would come to rule. The Old World was for the weak, the ignoble, the ungodly. It was a dark time in the minds of people who lived on Earth in the sinister year of 2068. They spat on the graves of those ancients with the words "God bless" or "Rest in peace" carved onto their headstones. They did not deserve to go to *their* "Heaven" nor rest peacefully beyond the grave. Indeed, New World citizens saw such people then as demons or walking forms of "cancer" that were entirely untaught of the new goddess who would come to be invented by an obscure, mysterious man.

Perhaps it was unavoidable–a sort of *the name of the game.* That is, people abandoning the old ways of life for a promised new one of endless prosperity and fairness. Has it not happened before, countless times as humanity evolved? It makes one think. One ideology pops up, only to be uprooted by another more "ethical" one. Hope and faith–the two greatest constructed forces–the grand weapons that allure all, more so than any amount of money or fame. They who utilize it correctly, gain the world. Unequivocally, no man in history would ever possibly fathom the dark tenets and creeds that would arise in the early 21st century.

It is likely about now that one asks themselves about the peculiar and mysterious man who started it all, as well as his faux goddess who outshadowed every previous idol. It will always remain an enigma to the lay people how it all began, but for those aristocrats and elites in the know, the plan was laid out quite cleverly, yet exceedingly simple.

A cunning and sly individual, Everett (as he was formally known) was he whom all this bizarre world gives its credit to. He invented the New Order–a new chapter of post-modernity. He would, in his devious mind, give birth to *Anathea*: the dangerous, maddening, powerfulest idea ever conceived. He would bring forth the new religion–the only acceptable one–with her, the thrice-high goddess Anathea: the make-believed woman in the sky who begot her chosen "son". Through Everette and his deity, the doctrines of an utter universal cult-of-personality would not only be tolerated, but encouraged.

Everett would later be called by a more pompous, persuasive title: *"Gabriel"*. He was the grand savior of not one country or peoples alone, but all who lived–whether human, plant, or creeping critter. Far more than Buddha, Jesus, Mohammad, and the like, he shone above all and higher in might than the sun over the Earth. According to the ragged, rigged society, he was the ultimate, all-knowing, ineffable ruler, under only his goddess–she who must be praised. He gave unto the people righteous dictatorship, pure regulation (under the guise of order), and a steel sword to cut down the foundation of his opponents.

The year was 2025 and the world, progressively having gotten worse over the centuries, finally succumbed to a disastrous and volatile state. Civil unrest was frequent, economies were in ruins, all while discontent and distrust of the government increased. If ever a more desperate time for a savior figure was needed, it was then–the year that the globe fell.

It was around those moments when a 30 year-old, extremely wealthy (and fairly famous) politician, Everett, came onto the scene. Both his lofty finances and as-of-then governance arose from corrupt dealing doing what other representatives asked him to do and say. He was a dreamer since childhood, but unlike a boy wanting to rise to the ranks of president, Everett wanted more than anyone had ever possessed. He fantasized about dictatorship and the potential to form the world in his image. Indeed, one could have called him a delusional narcissist and they would not be far off from the truth.

Over the course of about five years and when he was ripe in candidacy, he ruminated tirelessly on how one could accomplish such an undertaking. The stiff task would seem impossible with a normal functioning brain, but Everett's was made up of no less than greed, envy, and selfishness. It is a harsh thing to say, but his thirst for authority could not be quenched.

The solution came one day while writing a speech. The thought arose of how religious rhetoric generally had more effect than any one policy or persuasive official. No matter how well he could proclaim his political words to the public, and regardless of his affluence, he would never have a shot at rulership. It was at that moment that he created a being–a figment of a madman's psyche, as it were. This figment, *Anathea*, would be exceptionally pervasive in the hearts, eyes, and mouths of his future followers. He knew quite well, as do many leaders of cults, that when people are desperate, they will latch onto even the most absurd ideas. Such is especially easy when hope in those people had been absent and they hungered for salvation. He wanted Anathea to be their god, and he, her messiah.

The speech that he was to orate the next morning was one concerning the economy–one of the greatest predicaments and issues in his society; yet he, like most politicians, would be fruitless in his endeavors, as many sought against their own good and begged for more funding on social and infrastructure issues. He knew then, that night, the speech would mean nothing.

Having taken a gross number of theater classes, Everett was well-versed in the mannerisms which to display in order to catch people's attention. He was privy to speaking as a powerful, confident leader. Years of practice had sharpened his wits, and his grasp on the arts of persuasion were extraordinary. He could elegantly control his facial expressions, stand up straight, and flail his arms so as to dramatize his passion–yet not too much to seem over-confident.

Manic with his newfound thoughts, obsessed with his idealizations, he chose to throw away his former speech and write a new one: this one, describing the foreign, unknown goddess that was Anathea. He thought deeply about what he'd make of her. Would she be cunning, as himself? Merciful? Frightful? She was his creation and he had full reign over her attributes and will. No, he thought, she'd be as he imagined himself. She'd desire a new way of thinking; a new form of conduct and novel set of laws. Not to mention, he would have to include himself within it in some way.

The following day came and he was overly prepared. The piece he had put together was more akin to a gospel of sorts and far off from a typical speech. This time, he made sure to take away all banners and flags beside him, as well as any other needless things in order to make himself seem meek (which he surely was not). Anticipating it to be one of his grandest and most important speeches, the turnout was excellent. At least 2,000 people attended in a medium-sized stadium, clapping and cheering, unknowingly soon to be wrapped into a revolution. He presented himself differently from most occasions. Although secretly extremely calm and prepared, his disposition was that of elation and unruly excitement. Perhaps, of course, this was to make it seem as though he had a recent divine revelation. Inside of his mind, however, he laughed with a large grin, ready to pounce on the vulnerabilities of his current supporters.

He began the talk loudly and near-maniacal. Where his previous had been of a well-tempered man, this one was flamboyant and more of an expressive, yet vivid and coherent, nature.

He proclaimed, with a most honest temperament, that he had been receiving visions and apparitions for the last week from Anathea, the true and only god of the Earth. He spoke how she had hid the truth from mankind until the proper day when all would be in total anguish. According to Everett, all other deities and prophets were mere charlatans; those that weren't, were wrongfully guided by her and led astray. This was, of course, all foolery and a fabrication.

Naturally, the crowd, who had been enthusiastic and exuberant at first, became silent with confused faces. The assumption that many were disappointed, concerned, hateful, and even angry would not be unfounded. It was not at all what they expected.

After minutes upon minutes of pseudo-theological ramblings, he disclosed to them that he was the "chosen one" destined to lead humans to the "correct and noble" path of life. He said how she was his true mother who gave him soul and that she had guided him his whole life. Not fully having devised his own fiction, he spoke little about what Anathea wanted and how he'd change things if they listened. In reality, he was not as prepared as he should've been, but it did not matter.

The crowd's stance on the man quickly shifted and they swiftly, in a matter of half an hour, turned on him. Not that they were violent by any means, but boos and yelling began to overpower his voice. Fervent believers in his old, common, and lackluster discussions, many felt outraged at the sight of his inner feelings and goals. They (somewhat rightfully and with basis) assumed he had begun his whole political career for attention, only to say such things. Yet, there were those who felt as though he was not mentally stable, was in some kind of psychotic episode, and sympathized with him–thinking he needed help. They were not the majority.

Everett continued, but one-by-one, the people left in a hurried and disappointed fashion. It would've seemed then, that his chances of even garnering a sliver of triumph were destroyed; however, only a faint shed of disheartenment flickered in his heart. No, he was more determined than ever and knew he would have to be more prudent and deceitful. He did not flee the podium; instead, walking off gently, casually rotting his empathy and morality evermore within.

Over the next weeks, he came up with a brilliant plan. Brilliant, yet forbidding. Instead of a mere speech, he began writing his own "bible"--a manifesto of sorts, detailing his own sham religion in the image he saw fit. It would be called, *"The Will of Anathea"*. He laid out, in high description, the origin of Anathea, her desires, creation, and purpose. Most importantly, he followed this with his "New Testament", which would fully elaborate on his role as mankind's savior and destined ultimate king.

In a distant time ahead of this, a humble Peter would never know or fully understand the Old World before the dark creation of the goddess. Inconceivably foreign and alien settings would take a lifetime to digest; notwithstanding that all remnant notions such as Democracy, freedom, and independence, couldn't be found nor taught anywhere as it was; for none of such notions were presented in Everett's book.

To resume, however, it would do well to expound on this book and how it eventually rose to prominence before Peter's existence.

Now, in the 2020s, there was a wildly popular news outlet named the "New Times Gazette". Innocent enough at first. The man who owned it and its subsidiaries was the inconceivably rich John Greetly (who just so happened to be great friends with Everett). The latter man, knowing that if anyone could promote his book, it would have been Greetly. Therefore, he met with him, colluded, and made a proposition forthwith.

Everett gave his word that if Greetly published his book, gave it high attention and praise, he would pay the mogul a large sum of money. He also explained how he himself would make a media outlet after the book's success (given that it came to that), and he would place Greetly as his chief executive, head of his preachings.

To many, the deal sounded tasteful, but Mr. Greetly was reluctant. Indeed, naturally, he did not wish to risk tainting himself and his newspaper by commending a religious text, as it was taboo at the time. So, Everett left, and continued to contemplate on his fantastical plan.

Smart and nimble, he cooked up a scheme while lying in bed at nights. In his book, he told, in great detail, what would happen in the future. He intended it to appear as a prophecy and he himself being a beatific seer. In actuality, everything that would come to pass would be by his own workings and not "divine revelation" he was supposedly given.

The ploy would be simple, if it could be pulled off, and it well-exploited the fragile and raw vulnerabilities of their society. He wrote of how the United States would continue to be immensely divided and depraved until the point when a civil war broke out. The president would be overthrown, food shortages would occur, and a harsh depression would strangle the country. At that time (and until that point), many would rebuke and remain skeptical of Everett and

Anathea–seeing him as crazy or a fool. To prove that he was the true messiah, he said how he'd rise from the ashes and become prominent shortly afterwards. He would demonstrate how his prophecies were correct all along. He would then be charged with creating a New Order for mankind, as Anathea deemed it so. She would, as he always believed in her, prayed everyday, and was thus shown the future condition of the world.

Eventually, with deep consideration, Greetly accepted the offer (before the war) and agreed to publish the book, but not advertise widely. He wished for it to be in circulation, but not be generally known. It was after its distribution, that he quickly picked up his hammer to build his empire.

Everett began laundering money to a large mafia group that scourged the country. In disguise, he offered to pay them handsomely if they would disperse and burn down major food plants, as well as start fires sporadically in important places and cities. Obsessed with wealth, they agreed.

Soon after, Mr. Greetly jumped on board Everett's plan and threw himself wholeheartedly into the depths of his contemporary's wickedness. Thinking they could help each other even more, Greetly suggested they speak in private to known-corrupt James Whitwall–head of the U.S. Senate and Vice President.

As the food and resource supply chains were steadily becoming impeded, the two persuaded Whitwall to encourage as much government spending as possible to combat it. The consequences were horrendous for the common folk, while Whitwall would be applauded for his efforts.

Greetly, as eminent and respected as he was, then got into collaboration with other top dogs of mass media. He wanted them to create a false journalistic impression that a profusion of shortages (in all forms) would exponentially increase within the next six months. Although originating from the hidden mafias, the blame would be targeted at mysterious terrorists aided and funded by the president. Of course, the president had nought to do with any of it; but, being already very disliked and untrustworthy with low ratings and a bad reputation, the people were quick to center blame in his direction. Even fellow congressmen cast aspersions his way to hammer a nail in the coffin.

And to reiterate, this all was "prophesied" in Everett's *Will of Anathea,* and it was working effectively at the moment.

It was then that the media owners, under the spell of greed, fame, and power, created a host of slanderous and libelous accusations in order to present the president as being connected to the terrorists. They pushed the narrative hard, and the people, being the goats and perpetual followers of whatever the media shoved down their throats they were, lapped up the stories and became fueled by anger.

When a great deal of this was accomplished, and fear was in every corner of every city, the people began to panic and lose rationale. They started to buy every resource in bulk and, coupled with the massive spending and high inflation originating from the Federal Reserve, the huge depression foretold came fulfilled.

Outraged and with a feeling of grave betrayal, the people demanded the president be thrown in prison for his aid to the domestic terrorists. And yet, Congress was unable to find evidence of such dishonest dealings, and could not hold anything against him after impeachment. The people, on the other hand, desperate and poor, demanded action for the "injustices". They felt as though Congress had been covering for him and they themselves were connected. All of this had been laid out in detail in Everett's holy book.

With guns having been still legal, the people took to the streets. The time for peaceful protests had ended and riots befell every major city. Buildings, vehicles, forests, and even homes started to burn with each passing day, until the great rebellion was set up.

The president, obviously wanting to quell the masses and being Commander in Chief, sent in the National Guard to restore order. The people did not take kind to the move, instead raising their fists higher and screaming louder into the night. Seeing the president as a tyrant with his "personal army", the civil war was, for the most part, set about and fast in speed.

Once these things came to fruition, Greetly–along with the other moguls–immediately brought Everett's book into the limelight. It was indeed a most appropriate and proper time. Large scale reporting told how the book "predicted" the events that took place. They praised Everett, as though he was the only true prophet, and the mysterious being known as Anathea should have been given credence. The more attention they got, the greater their push towards declaring him her chosen son.

The book was sold in droves–far more than any previous one of the last half millennium before. Eyes smokey with desperation, they could not help but see him the way he announced himself to be. He was like no other prophet of the past with vague sayings and occasionally incorrect predictions. He was too accurate to be disbelieved.

The government had essentially been abolished about that time. Many officials had been assassinated (including the president), hanged in the streets, or disposed of in numerous ways. For a small minute, anarchy was briefly the norm. All–whether soldiers, children, elders, or highly religious people–began to consider Everett and marvel at his charisma. Both sides of the war slowly lowered their weapons and turned to him, trusting that he would enforce order again–a "better one", as he said.

As there were no mythologies about Anathea, Everett conjured up any ideas he desired and possessed full control. He proclaimed her wills, how all other gods and goddesses were mere made-up puppets to her–the highest unimaginable being.

Within only a year, a new government had been universally accepted, with he, their de facto (at the time) leader. He was led as a duck to water in his ambitions–accomplishing the first steps he had laid out with fair ease. It sounded promising at first, and the vast majority helped facilitate the change. Little did they know just how far the so-called New Order of the refreshing

New World would go, and how powerful the man known as Everett, who changed his name to *Gabriel*, meaning "God is my strength" and his peculiar goddess would eventually become.

CHAPTER 2

Power By Whips

Anathea was noticeably distinct from every past god and goddess. It is, therefore, all the more surprising that past religious adherents easily converted to such a strange and different ideology/teachings. Perhaps, a deal of her success came from her enigmatic character–being a god that united all previous ones. For, according to "Gabriel", it was she who created all other religions to lead men astray. The goal of this was to, in a way, "trick humans"; that they would have freewill, requiring them to follow their own faith and piety. Only then could they receive salvation. She wanted the most devout neophytes to find her on their own accord.

However, the majority of the people's transitions was irrefutably due to Gabriel. His predictions of the 2020s were not the only ones to come true. For the next forty years, he would continue along the lines of his past deceptions and pre-plan staged events, evermore convincing all that he was the greatest prophet. As no one had ever seen such a precise character, they could not accept that he was a mountebank–even the slightest. No, his insight was simply too much to be gainsaid.

Later on, he would perform "miracles", as well. He would occasionally give speeches and declare that thunder and lightning would strike at any moment. Behind the scenes and the stage, a powerful futuristic technology was able to produce an electric shock into the air while a bomb-like noise went off. Just as equal, he would give paid individuals a sort of disease. The affected people would publicly beg Gabriel that he use his powers to heal them. It would be then that he provided them a secret cure and they suddenly became healthy once again. Indeed, part of these miracles could only be done decades after his prominence, but many did not. What mattered was wit, power, and wherewithal. With those three features, nothing was out of his reach.

The purpose of humans, according to the "righteous" dictator, was to essentially be slaves to the goddess. They were, in a way, created for her entertainment via her egocentrism. The modus operandi was that humans were supposed to be *tested*. She was a selfish god who desired worship, and only those who prevailed in returning to look and gaze unto her in faith would be saved. Those who could not find the correct path would suffer reincarnation on Earth (which was Hell), until the point where they–in truth, *gave in*– worshiped her, and would be raptured, resting in Heaven with her in neverending pleasure. Of course, to any sane individual, the concept of creating for entertainment seems absurd, but so were the thoughts of absurd, abused minds of Gabriel's followers.

True and without error, people are gullible. Every person believes their fellow neighbor to be less of a free-thinker than themselves, yet it is a fallacy. It was apparent to anyone before the universal doctrine of control arose, but in the Anathean times, the concept of gullibility did not exist. Each person, no matter who, fully gave themselves to her and her son, and all knew they were right. Also, naivety and gullibility implies *individuality*–that each person is more sovereign in their thinking than another. This was utterly not the case. Individualism had long been dead. It was seen as an attribute of a high ego or that they were rebellious towards being one with Anathea and other believers. Oneness was the key. People were not allowed–and definitely not encouraged–to think or behave differently from their peers. They fervently believed that the only way to salvation and eternal freedom was if they all came together, united, and had exactly the same minds. It was group-think, and to think otherwise was heretical. Gabriel was the ideal god-king, a golden idol; the nobelist thing to do was emulate him.

The early days of the regime were slow, yet quick in the grand scale of history. People were left confused and bewildered that their prophesied messiahs did not return when the world was in turmoil. They lost faith, but faith is a hard thing to let go and it took some years. Gabriel brought order onto them when there was only chaos and darkness–exactly like the saviors promised in every religion. Many believed he was right and that their religions had somehow been corrupted over the millennia. These ideas were already common in the 2020s, so it took little to be fully accepted.

After about 2035, Anathea-ism was rampant and nearly all believed in it globally; the only exceptions being the elderly who remembered the before-times and were "stubborn in their erroneous ways". They quickly became outnumbered and had no choice but to agree and keep silent, lest they be punished and ostracized.

There were many issues Gabriel addressed other than religion. Economics and social matters were the second main focuses. He knew that to break the people down and give themselves fully over to him, he'd have to redefine and alter what it meant to be free. The first was Capitalism.

Though secretly agreeing with it, he made his point known that Capitalism was greedy, as was the desire to earn money, start one's own businesses, and freely purchase one's needs and wants. Many of the Old World already thought this, but he would take it to the extreme. The want for anything that another didn't already have was "evil consumerism"; that they were self-seeking, selfish, and wanted more than others for a sense of power. Despite only a small percentage of the people being like that, he convinced everyone that they were being unfair, egocentric, and trying to be better than others.

Gabriel explained that Anathea was a cunning goddess who believed in fairness and equality for all. She found that any who had even one grape more deserved none. If one had a home with an extra bedroom, they deserved no home at all.

Hence, along these lines, Gabriel created his own form of government and economy. They were essentially connected, so the word "economy" ceased to be spoken of. This new system and way of the New World would be called "*Whipism*"--literally meaning "Power By The Whip". It was a sort of extreme Facism, in between Capitalism, Socialism, and Communism. The concept of Whipism was to *whip* (either literally or metaphorically) or smite dissidents who went against the Order. The past judicial systems of the past were no longer needed; law would be enforced by the whips of the military. The evil essence of this should properly be expounded on later.

Economically, he sought that the government (with he as its head) be in full control of matters of the job market and money control. He preached equal pay for all—regardless of jobs, choice, or abilities–and universal income. For a few years, this worked as he planned, but it quickly began to fall apart and he was forced to dissolve it. The main (among many) problems were incentives. Droves of citizens ceased to work, either because they were already getting free money, or couldn't get the job they wanted. Part of the latter was the fact that there were no inclinations to do good in one's job since there was no possibility of promotions or chances to get high wages. They could also not get fired.

Instead, the system changed soon after. People would be provided all commodities: housing, food, water, medicines, jobs, etc. The caveats being that they were required to attend work, put absolute faith in his governance, obey stricter laws, and be happy with little without demanding more. Money was done away with, and a type of labor-backed currency (without actually currency) was the new structure.

Meanwhile, he appointed a handful of very high people who were already rich elites in the Old World who knew how to persuade people easily. They were obviously Aristocrats, but he said how they were his "top disciples" who would therefore help him rule. Mindless sheep, the people fell for it without an iota of questions. Behind curtains, the Aristocrats would become extraordinarily rich off the people's labor, as they took in what they could get without working themselves. Their work was "overseeing order".

Raving, joyful, and frenzied with their new free resources they were in desperate need of, the people spewed out more and more praise to their dictator. They willingly wanted to hand over all power to him and have him make decisions for them. They were blinded by his words. Since their items were free, they assumed that was the definition of "freedom". The word "liberty" was never spoken in polite conversations. He had distorted that word also, to mean *people who rule in ignorance and without governmental leadership.*

Not long after this, sociology was the next target. Indeed, resources are the primary (and most important) concern of the people and the first thing that ought to be dealt with. No matter how evil a parent is nor how maltreated the child, the kid will always run back to them for food and shelter when desperate. Given the people didn't admire Gabriel (which was utterly not the case), once he dominated the supply chains and suffocated every facet of society with his cold metallic hands, they would have no choice but to obey.

Whipism was already turning remarkably successful, but the king would need to be more forceful when it came to shaping the minds who were then dependent on him. He would need Whipism to have far more implications than before, and the italicized "whip" would need emphasis.

Like Anathea herself, it was an entirely new concept, and Gabriel had supreme authority over saying what it meant. A level of control never seen before, it was an amalgamation of all past evils. It entailed extreme income inequality (unknown to the public), drastic destruction of past information (works of religion, myth, legend, non-fiction, and literary pieces discussing morality, in particular), and most frightening, the creation of a new *"correct language"*. Many other aspects would also need rendering or interference. Births, food, land, weapons, etc., would require extreme regulation or abolishment.

Perhaps more dangerous than any of the aforementioned, a social credit system was put into place. Those who followed Anathea-ism well, helped the government, walked in the law, reported *old ways*, and never complained, had theirs raised. By doing so, they'd receive greater daily rations of drugs, Rapts, food, and water. They may have also been bumped to a more favorable occupation. Those who had their's lowered would be punished from such and likely *whipped* into place–however it was defined in that moment in time.

CHAPTER 3

Peter's Dystopia

Peter stood by the window, looking out into the gloomy, smog-ridden city, loathing attending school yet another day. A self-effacing, innocent 24 year-old boy, Peter was a bird who'd never know the freedom of a blue sky. His disposition often showed happiness, but inside, his heart was melted, bones out of joint with unease, and his eyes weary of seeing darkness.

He lived in a humble, old and worn down home (appointed by the government, of course) in a small city in Northwestern Washington. Truly, his city was less dystopian than say, Seattle below, but still under the firm grasp of the Order. Nowhere in the world (especially America) had autonomy. Neither states, nor provinces, nor countries remained separated. Cameras and microphones still hid in every crevasse, and World Guards continually patrolled the streets. There was nowhere to flee, nowhere to run.

Although in his mid-twenties, Peter was still preparing to go to school. The education system of the New World was quite distinct from the old one. Children were required to begin attending at the age of four until they turned 25 when their brains were fully developed. Therefore, Peter was in his 20th grade and set to graduate the following year–which he was greatly looking forward to.

Peter was a stranger in Anathean society. He was born into it and never knew anything of the past; nor was he permitted to learn about it, even if he wanted to. And yet, he had always felt ill of the regime, as though there was something wrong and evil about it. In his heart, it was not a utopia as others told him, but a prison wherein impenetrable, sufferable, and escapeless. He longed for a way out of it, yet not fathoming a life any different. He knew neither what freedom meant, other types of governments, nor a life outside of the hallowed Anathea. He was led into captivity at birth, not knowing what independence nor self-sufficiency was. He could never taste the sweet wine that was emancipation, nor savor the fruits of liberation. Yet, somewhere in the back of his mind, he faintly had an imaginary glimpse of such a life. He'd ponder daily on a world without universal, psychosocial, iniquity. Other than Janet and his father, there were no others who could relate or comfort his thoughts. Still, no matter the amount of propaganda and rhetoric, he held onto his doubts and dreams–whatever they were.

He was an only-child and longed for a sibling–being regularly lonely. His mother had died many years prior after a bad spout of pneumonia. Severe ailments like that were common, due to frequent power outages that left homes without heat in the Winter months. He was hence left with his father, George, whom he always lived with.

Thankfully, his parents (like himself) never bought into the doctrines of Anathea. They raised him to be deeply skeptical of the goddess and Gabriel but, by the nature of eternal societal influence, he knew only of them. His parents were alive in the Old-World, but only before adulthood when they conceived. They therefore vaguely remember the old ways and could not teach him as much as they wished.

Naturally, the family had lived in perpetual fear for most of their lives. Regardless if one breaks (one of extraordinarily many) laws, being known as an anti-Anathea-ist or disobeying the dictator would surely put one on a watchlist and have their social credit score suffer a massive blow. They made sure to keep all of their discussions to themselves and only speak when they were absolutely sure they would not be observed. It was everyone's duty to report Old World speech or illegal talk. The goal of this, as one could imagine, was to instill mass paranoia in the global public. Paranoia and habitual anxiety was a great method of keeping "order"--perhaps even better than the fear of whips or prisons. The great, ultimate weapon of fear was the people's willing belief in a sick dogma that went against them. They created their own Hell and frolicked in it. One didn't need to go out and murder or rob; they needed only to say the wrong things or commit the most petty of crimes for who knows how many lashes or worse.

His father was a very kind man, yet many a time kept to himself. Peter never thought much of it, but the truth was likely that he was depressed. It's only natural when one is on death row and unsure if they'll go to Heaven without committing a crime. The father and son's relationship could not have been better and they knew they would have to rely on each other more than ever after his mother's passing.

Something of note was the fact that Peter's father had never been employed. This was very odd in the Anathean world, as all were required to–save those who lost all privileges of living and were forced to starve and dwell on the streets. Anyone who did not work were commonly seen as wastes or garbage that lowered the integrity of Gabriel's regime. They were looked down upon as *cancers,* only consuming without producing; they therefore did not support Anathea's creation and work towards progress, but instead were "gluttonous", feasting off of her resources, and abusing the labors that others endured without giving any effort themselves to help their fellow humans. Such people were often shunned or physically abused on the streets out of fear that they'd set a bad example and persuade others to not work.

Strangely, neither Peter nor his father actually knew why he couldn't work and contribute. His father was born with a "weak" heart, so they speculated it had something to do with that. Thankfully, it was only after he was a baby that they discovered the condition, else he would have been euthanized.

Still, it was odd as the Department of Labor did not value life nor equity. When a man and woman desired a child, they would first need approval from the Department of Breeding. If granted and approved, they would go in, each for an examination. They would be evaluated on appearance and mental health. Any who were not prime human stock were rejected and declared *"unreproducible"*. Only those with the absolute best genetics were permitted to breed and aid the population. Naturally, then, Peter and his family (as most) were quite beautiful and healthy. If a baby was illegally born or born with unforeseen defects, they would immediately be euthanized. It can be assumed that somehow his father slipped under the rug and his heart did not turn feeble until later. If he had not, there would be no telling of dear Peter and his experiences.

Peter packed up his things and began his walk to school. On his way–like every other day–he observed the repellent scenes and dreary sights that were the setting. For being Gabriel's "utopia", there were no massive ornate buildings in the city–at least not his. Since all in his neighborhood (yet also in many other places) were poor in resources and social credit, most buildings and homes were small and desolate in appearance.

Tall buildings and obelisks-like towers scraping the sky filled the city. The buildings shone many lights across them and had fire and smoke coming out the tops of them. The means of creating clean energy certainly existed, but due to the poor state of the "economy", fossil fuels remained the mainstay. The buildings required great quantities of power–more so of past ones–and were hence powered by coal and oil.

They looked quite beautiful at night; lighting up the atmosphere with glowing embers; yet, suffocating and filthy at the same time, with smog lingering about at every hour of each day.

Atop the towers were massively oversized cameras–much like evil eyes of myth. They watched all the happenings of the city with high definition. They were able to track and monitor the whole populace: surveying and profiling the people with magnificent supercomputers/databases.

Nevertheless, gigantic embroidered posters featuring either Gabriel or Anathea hung on every third structure. Something like oversized holographic television screens were placed along the streets, constantly airing propaganda and speeches by the savior or his Aristocrats. Although these items were spread apart, others would not be. It was utterly mandatory that every household have a flier with the major laws plastered to their doors and the holy flag of Anathea be hung off the roofs.

The more official government buildings were not run down, but looked like colossal concrete prisons surrounded by razor-wire fencing with World Guards roaming the grounds. The schools looked about the same as those, but to a slightly lesser degree. Friendly appearances meant nothing.

Peter dreaded his school (really, all for that matter) and perhaps even feared it, to a degree. Private schools were not legal, and every public school had to follow the same criteria and governmental orders. Unlike in the Old World when Democracy ruled, parents had absolutely no say in the children when at school. The teachers (who were seen as direct lines between Gabriel and his messages to children) were in charge of indoctrinating the students and raising them to be noble, compliant citizens.

It was very easy to see the government hold on schools the moment Peter sat at his desk and took out his books–one of them being the Will of Anathea. Every single one was written after the New World had been laid out and were all written by the dictator's Aristocrats. Any book before the New Order was thoroughly outlawed and those found with them could face long prison sentences or even be sent to slave camps for re-education.

The New World schools were much like military boot camps. The goal was essentially to "break down" the students, destroy their sense of individuality, and mold them into righteous, united followers. The students would have to speak the *correct language* and act in accordance with submissiveness. As such, gloves were off there, and to get in trouble did not simply mean detention.

The daily lessons pertained most to the Order and how it functioned, as well as studying the theology of the goddess. Things like science, art, history, and math, were rarely taught. History in particular, when discussed, was the most altered since the 2020s. Nothing taught was true, not in the slightest. Stories of the past were changed to fit Gabriel's agenda. There were pieces, such as the existence of other ancient religions, that were stated, but everything about them and their origins was fabricated. "Inspirational" posters were taped to the walls, some reading things like: *"Do your part, educate your friends to be saved"* and *"The only way to accomplish peace is to whip the terrorist unbelievers in shape"*.

When the teacher spoke, none were allowed to go against her methods or words. One may have asked questions, but they dared not contradict the answers. The same went for the homework and tests. If one wrote an *incorrect* essay or a righteous one, yet with *incorrect language*, they would have to be punished.

School was the predominant reason why Peter battled inside his mind and did not understand his own brain. He knew he was taught a lie, but they had planted the counterfeit knowledge in him nearly every day since birth. When one knows (awarely) only falsehoods and has no means to find the truth, it drives that person insane. For Peter, it brought more sadness than infuriation. He simply didn't know the truth, but knew deep down that he'd have to find it—even if it killed him.

Janet often sat beside him in class and she was his best (perhaps only) friend. Like him, she was, for better or worse, a rebel who went against the New Order, their ruler, and Anathea. They frequently read illegal books together when they could find them or watch forbidden old films in secrecy. It therefore was that Peter did have a slight peek into the Old World, but still not knowing exactly how it functioned or what people believed. Most books were simply math textbooks or useless how-to's, while the few movies were romances and cartoons. Even still, the films made it seem like a utopia or kind of Earthly heaven—even if the people didn't appreciate it at the time.

Janet and Peter were inseparable when together. They knew each other since their fourth year and clicked right away with their shared interests. How they came to be partners in crime was fuzzy. No one would ever try to speak illegally with another, as they would fear being reported. Somehow Janet felt the same way, which was strange since her parents were about as fervent Anathea-ists as they could get. As such, their activities would have to be concealed at Peter's house. In fact, he invited her to come over after class that day to do such activities.

Before class had ended, the teacher had asked Peter to stay after class. That was always a bad sign and Peter grew worried that he had somehow slipped up and went against the rules. He could only imagine what she'd do to him if that was the case.

He was pleasantly surprised when, instead of being scolded, he actually received compliments on his work over the year. She said his grades had been doing excellent and the government had begun to take notice. As he felt he put minimum effort into his work, saying and writing only what he thought she wanted to hear, he couldn't believe it when she said the Department of News was offering him an internship.

One may assume the position to be quite prestigious for a young man still in school, but Peter was, not in fact, entirely happy with it. The Department of News was the one and only news outlet in the world and it was wholly run by the elites. It was unquestionably and solely a propaganda medium–relaying Gabriel's messages to a blind citizenry.

Interestingly, the word "propaganda" no longer existed–despite its widespread use. Instead, it was called under a euphemism: "awareness announcements". The people were supposed to be attentive to *things that mattered*, whether good or bad. Fundamentally, awareness announcements would portray *ideal thoughts* and *noble ways of acting*. The people heard and read them as gospel.

Unlike jobs, internships were allowed to be chosen, accepted, or denied. Peter, as much as he despised the department and didn't want to go, reluctantly accepted. He believed it was the only way of raising his credit score enough to take care of his father and Janet. He dreamt of raising them out of poverty and being able to obtain the high-end resources that others in the media had.

The two met later that night at Peter's. He had a small crawl space beneath the floor of a back room which they'd go into. They always made sure to hide it and cover it with a rug. It was the only place, even in their own homes, where they could be safe. Still, if raids occurred, they have to make sure to be extra cautious.

The space was small and low in height, lit up by a few electronic lanterns. The walls and floor were made of dirt, so they had a thick blanket to sit on; not the most comfortable of places, but to them, it was fully worth it. The technology they had down there would have been unrecognizable and primitive to the New Worlders. He had an antique non-holographic television that he was able to power by homemade wiring. As well as that, there was a small, shabby DVD player with only a couple disks. There were other foreign and strange paraphernalia. Many would have been mere collectables or common day items in the past, but it was highly treasured by the two of them. Coins, pamphlets, electric toy cars that no longer worked, and obsolete, rusted batteries, were others, to name a few.

Peter put on a very old film called, "A Streetcar Named Desire" They'd seen it a million times over but found solace in it and made them dream of being one of the characters. Movies no longer lived–only the Autocrat's news.

As it played, they visualized freedom and longed for escape. They'd often discuss what they'd do, where'd they go, and how they'd live in a place without Anathea-ism. How could they escape Gabriel's reach? They could only dream. His regime was not limited to one place; he controlled the entire planet. He was the worldwide leader and no other governments–save his–existed.

Although not wanting to, Peter was an honest man and confided in Janet his internship. She was not pleased with it, but after he explained he was doing it for them, she agreed he should try it out. He felt a small amount of shame working in propaganda, but if he didn't do it, someone else would, and therefore nothing would change and he had nothing to lose.

Janet gently rested her head on his lap and slowly dozed off to sleep while he continued to watch the movie. A one hundred year-old movie, it may as well have been archaic, and was odd being two-dimensional, but he could somehow relate to those times more so than his own which he'd grown up in.

Strange, it portrayed someone going from prosperity to descending to a lower class. Despite fantasizing about the opposite, he could admire that. It inspired him to appreciate his situation and what little he had, even if it wasn't pleasurable. Sometimes the richest of men would be those without money. Peter wasn't an elite, but rich with knowledge and goodness in his heart and mind.

Quietly, he too drifted off to sleep, comforted that his friend was there to keep him company in a place so despondent.

CHAPTER 4

Department of Indoctrination

It was a few days later when Peter was to go to the Department of News for the first time. To someone of the Old World, two days would sound quite quick from the moment of his offer, but things moved amazingly fast in Anathean society. Perhaps the reason for it was to "throw the people in a loop", as it were. That is, make everything seem to move at breakneck speed in order that their attention spans are shortened and they soon forget anything of the past six months. That method was already at work in the 20s, with new major events occurring daily. It may have also been the fact that they did not want Peter to heavily consider working with them or not. Humans tend to get more cautious, skeptical, and reasonable when they have time to think things over. They wanted Peter to be a drone–not a freethinker or inquisitor of his heinous duties.

He awoke early and threw on his all-black torn jumpsuit. Everyone was required to wear them while working. The pitch blackness of it symbolized that humans were the darkness in Anathea's creation, and they ought to have been aware of it and humiliated. To the people, self-hatred masquerading as penitence was ideal and the norm. They found it correct to be ashamed of being on Earth and not in her Heaven. It was only the Aristocrats that could wear white garments; with Gabriel, clothed in gold.

On his way there, he stopped at a rationing post for some Rapts. Nicknamed "Happy Capsules", Rapts–which could "rapture" people–were drugs with heavy antidepressant effects. A mixture between countless pharmaceutical ingredients, hard opioids, and low doses of ecstasy, they were the ideal drug of choice for most people.

An important footnote in the exposition of the New World was drug use. None, not even the strongest, were illegal. In fact, the government handed out drugs as though they were candy and constantly encouraged their use. To the normal man, it's obvious to understand why this was. The people were supposed to be kept happy at all costs. Even with their religion, it would have been all too easy to get low and depressed with having little to nothing. Indeed, a limbless man would not bat an eye at his condition nor feel any sense of indignation if he were constantly on heroin or the like. A young girl who still feared death would be infinitely elated on her deathbed if under the influence of Rapts.

As such, the drugs could easily also be used against the people. Given their social credit score lowered and they were declined a daily amount of Rapts, they'd shape up quickly and fear ever losing their doses again. It was almost like the threat of prison to them. Most could not bear the horrendous withdrawals.

As many of the drugs had intense psychoactive properties, it was commonplace for people to experience "visions" or "divine influence" when under their spell. Like shamans of the past, they believed the drugs opened their eyes wider and they could *feel* Anathea's presence even more. Mass placebo and hysteria was very real.

Peter did not have an addictive personality nor ever wanted to start taking them, but the urge and peer pressure around him would persuade anyone. Oddly, people who refused them were looked at as strange or suspicious–as though they were against the recommendation of Gabriel for whatever reason. Neighbors may've assumed such people did not want to be happy, as though they disregarded the Order and wanted to be aware of just how sinister it was–not desiring to be in a pleasurable trance while standing upon the gallows.

If they wanted to be hateful or sad on Anathea's world, then they would not go to Heaven where happiness dwelt, according to others. *They rejected the gifts of drugs and thereby rejected Gabriel and the goddess' presents. Drugs bring one closer to the firmament, for they bring one joy and act kinder to their fellow peers–a trait the goddess rejoices at.* Madness, indeed.

As any psychiatrist of the Old World could assume, there were countless "crazy" folks in the streets; having become insane due to psychosis brought on by the horrible substances.

Directly following this, Peter stopped at the Community Pantry. It was like an Old World store, but more of a resource and food bank, as money was absent. On the front doors, before entering, one could not help but see the posters that stated the laws and some of their statutes. Once entered, he again saw the two sections; a sight he was most familiar with.

Now, the Community Pantries were divided into two parts: one, called the *High-Side*, was only for the elites, while the *Low-Side* was for the common, poor folk.

The High-Side, as one may expect, was filled with the highest quality healthy food, drinks, medicines, alcohol, and appliances. Meanwhile, the Low-Side contained rotten and moldy vegetables/fruits, exceedingly unhealthy food containing many chemicals and preservatives, low-quality medicines, and cheap appliances. All sweets there were filled with artificial sweeteners, as sugar was a hard commodity to come by–available only to the most consecrated.

There were daily limits on the amount of resources one could get. Those with the higher credit scores/elites, would be permitted to acquire more, while most (who did not) could only shop on the lower isles.

Food of the High-Side was utterly exquisite, made by some of the best chefs, and were of the highest quality. They deserved better lives because of their saintly piety. Some of them would contain special chemicals that affected the taste buds and made the food even more decadent, opposed to the others which harmed people's health and could make them sick.

Naturally, anyone caught stealing from the High-Side was acutely punished depending on the severity of their crime and what they took. Likely, they would be banned permanently or suspended from the Pantry–essentially left to fend for themselves, live at the mercy of others' charity, or starve. It was by no means easy to get away with it. Cameras–like everywhere else–were planted all throughout the buildings to monitor how often one came in, how much they took, and the stickers on their chests that told which side they could shop in.

There was a sort of caste system that existed. Those with good credit were seen as having been reincarnated into a good life because they were good in their past one and thus close to entering Heaven. On the other hand, those poor and without good credit were scrutinized and not valued as greatly. They would "require more time to leave Earth". As a consequence of this, it was okay to be harsher on them, as it would put them more "in shape" so they could be raptured.

Afterwards, he again began on his way. As he strolled, he noticed the ordinary sights. Massive floating 3D televisions were attached to most buildings and posts. At every hour, both day and night, they showed montages of Gabriel saving the human race, encouraging people to stay happy, trust in him, and therefore receive salvation. Some were videos of him giving imposing speeches amidst roaring crowds, while others were him in temples giving sermons and masses with his "disciples" standing beside him praying.

Commercials were no longer a thing, but there were occasional screenings of the sort. They showed popular advocates coaxing the population to get their drugs, go to their jobs, be humble (happy with being poor), be dependent on the venerable government, read, and do their duties of reporting suspicious behaviors.

Along the streets were stationed Guards who ambled about, watching attentively to beat and whip any who stepped out of line. They looked extremely menacing, yet had smiles on their faces. They were drunk with power; sadists excited to punish any who appeared distant from the Order. They loved their job and fed off of the pain of others.

When he finally arrived at the scary, intimidating building, he was taken to a small room. He was met with seven other suave-looking men who sat across from him. They had the most serious and stern faces, free of any possible emotion other than perhaps disinterest.

Although it was said to be an "interview", Peter felt it was more akin to an interrogation. They gave difficult questions to answer and did not respond with a sliver of feedback or commentary. They were probing him with questions, digging deep into his mind about what he truly believed. They were no-nonsense men.

Of course, Peter said only what they wanted to hear in the most earnest tone. He had become a fairly good professional liar, but those detectives were far more skilled and could sniff out any who went against their interests.

They asked his opinions on the government, leader, news, and his expected duties. It's a difficult thing to lie to that degree without slipping up, but he managed to do it as best as he could. In truth, it didn't matter if they rejected him; he'd be in the same situation as he was before and there almost certainly wouldn't be any consequences. Hence, he didn't take it too seriously.

They all got up at the same time without muttering a word, and then left the room to convene. As minutes upon minutes passed, Peter grew nervous and speculated about what they must've been thinking. Surely, regardless of if they were doubtful, he'd simply return home, but he still dreamt of helping Janet and his father.

To his surprise, they offered him the position once they returned. Although he was excited, they still showed no facial expressions whatsoever and immediately told him to start that minute. He was taken up to another floor, down a corridor, into a very large, bustling room. Oddly, the room was intensely silent and eerie. People ran around all over the place, but made not a peep other than stomping feet and continuous keyboard strokes.

They all sat writing articles at their desks painlessly and rapidly without a moment of breaktime. Peter admired the silent, calm nature of the work, but couldn't help but possess a feeling of uncanniness, knowing he couldn't socialize and be required to publish lies without any help.

For the time being, he was directed to copyright and help advertise news. Seemed simple, he thought. Yet, in actuality, he was to make opinion pieces (the only correct ones, mind you) and spread articles concerning "terrorist" activities. It was not his cup of tea, but he wasn't expecting the job to be different or about truths.

The definition of terrorism had changed since the Old World era. Essentially, anything/anyone that went against the regime was considered terrorism: for, opposing views or actions against Anathea brought terror and fear to the people and globe. They dismayed the citizenry and gave the sense that their goal was to overthrow Gabriel's creation. Obviously, this was usually not the case. Dissidents would, in fact, fantasize about changing the populace and taking down the dictator, but they would not act on violence. They would stand no chance, even if they wanted to. More often than not, it was usually labeled *religious terrorism*, adding an extra word to make it seem even more dangerous and against the people's interests.

Peter was given an extensive list of illegal words to examine when writing, so he would not break the law or anger the people. Although already aware of most of them, there were so many that one single person could not always know each one. It was for that reason, that if one did not know if a word was *correct*, they'd simply not speak.

To name a few: animals, were *lower lifeforms*; humans, were *inclining slaves*; women, were *pink people* (the color of the womb); men, were *procreators*; laws, were *healthy rules*; criminals, were *demons*; any other governments, were *tyrannies*; Old World politicians, were *snakes*; disagreements, were *divisive hatred*; prisons/slave camps, were *re-education centers*; whips, were *virtuous disciplinary tools*; illegal actions, were *unholy deeds*; families, were *familiar pods*; and so on…

Almost no one remembered or were aware of the Old Language, so it wasn't exactly common to get in trouble for it. Usually, if one were caught speaking the incorrect words, they were either very old or had read outlawed books. The latter was the more serious crime and the repercussions for being caught with said paraphernalia was grave.

Gabriel knew that the only way to get people perfectly devoted to him, was to erase every possible thing about the Old World. One purpose of the New Language was to prevent people from understanding old books/movies, even if they discovered them. The people would not even be able to interpret the fairly foreign speech, making it difficult to change their minds or ideas. Words, or rather language for that matter, that described candid truth were the most feared, but the people didn't realize what accurately described objective reality–thus being ignorant of truth twice-fold.

Luckily for Peter and Janet, his father did know Old Speech, having grown up with it to teach them, and observing illegal texts/movies strengthened their knowledge of original English vocabulary. It was, however, a small curse, as it made the three even more furious about their society and they had to watch their utterances more so than others.

At any rate, Peter would continue in his routine at the Department for another few weeks when his boss, Mr. Hemot, raised and allocated him to the position of assistant editor. Unlike before, Peter enjoyed the job–at least, as much as he could. He'd no longer have to advertise and spread fake, blown-up news. It was a fairly easy task, and he need not have paid much attention to the context and message; rather simply the grammar and words. He was not an expert in the English language nor excellently privy in literacy, but he must have been seen as such to the board. They took a liking to him and saw writing/proofreading as a gift of his. He certainly wasn't going to decline their fanciness towards him.

Many of the pieces he reviewed were of citizens caught with illegal items, but also some of unauthorized, Anti-Anathea-ist speeches or uprisings. The media made the rebellions look utterly horrific and dangerous, which was odd, as no one often had seen anything of the sort in real life; yet, there were plenty of interviews scattered throughout them to back them up, so they could not be disregarded. Of course, the interviewees made their experiences sound petrifying–almost too frightening–and caught Peter's suspicions, but he had to accept them as factual.

Many of such criminal activities were usually, among many other reasons, to rile up people's support of increasing their already large military to quell dissent. The people were completely ignorant that they were going against their own interests and losing even more control. Safety and security: the best of promises, and easiest mode of taking away rights.

And yet it was, that as Peter loathed his job more and more, knowing he was doing wrong, he began to slack in his workings, giving slightly more credit to the criminals and Anti-Anathea-ists over the weeks. The bosses and chief editors immediately noticed and scolded him harshly. He was demanded to add more propagandic sentences and declarations in the articles, with progressively more extravagant headlines. Instead of, "Terrorists At The Valley Courts", he would change it to, "BREAKING: Treacherous Terrorists Armed With Heavy Weapons Seek Overthrow!". Without choice, he obeyed.

He was on his way to school again one day, when he met Janet beforehand. She had wanted to tell him something important. Assuming it had to do with breaking the rules, Peter took her to the backside of the building where no other people could see them and they didn't have to fear being caught.

Peter's face lit up when she brought out a strange little book from out of her backpack. It was authored by a mysterious writer named "Friedrich Nietzche". Neither of the two had heard of him nor seen such a philosophical book. Out of fear, Peter immediately told her to hide it somewhere where others couldn't find it. She couldn't risk putting it in her backpack (as shakedowns were a frequent occurrence) so Peter convinced her to stick it underneath a garbage can until after school.

When Peter asked where she found it, she explained how she was exploring an old shack on the outskirts of town, fairly deep into the woods. The entire city was surrounded by steel fences, but she stumbled upon a cut in it in order to get through. She told how it was a very peculiar place–looking out of time. There were other *uncommon things* secretly stashed within it and she wanted to return.

They both were extremely eager to open the book, but knew they'd have to wait and with caution. Old World books, of all forms, were illegal, but philosophical and religious ones, especially so. Charges could range from three to four times as high.

Peter, although calm tempered, was fairly angered that she'd be so foolish to bring it to school. No one would be sympathetic to them if they were seized. The students were no less dangerous than the faculty. They would report them at once.

Speaking of writings, she brought up his work and articles. She said how she was disappointed in them and that Peter was doing a terrible thing. It made him feel bad–her thinking of him like that–, but he knew she was right. He had always appreciated her honesty and integrity, so for her to tell him the truth made him love her even more. Still, the only excuse he could muster was that it'd help both of them in the long run and raise them in the ranks of society. He couldn't shake the feeling, however, that he may have been selfish. Was it worth harming society and corrupting the peoples' minds for the sake of better living only for Janet, his father, and himself? He loved them more than anyone, but they could still get by, even if he quit. She thought he was being unreasonable, and a part of him couldn't deny that as the truth. He knew she was often more down-to-Earth than himself–more grounded and stubborn in her morals.

School began shortly afterwards and their first period was "Civility Class". The purpose of the course was to *make good citizens* (really make compliant and obedient without question). They would discuss Gabriel and his disciples' holiness, Anathea, and the proper ways of life; but more often than not, Whipism was the predominant subject.

They watched a government-backed video that day, teaching them in-depth about the doctrine of it, how to follow it, and why it was important. It spoke about how Anathea was a strict and stringent lord who demanded discipline and rigorous compliance. She was unrelenting and wrathful towards those who deviated from her will and order. Under Whipism, people were told that one had a duty to follow the rules of her and the dictator whithersoever they went; for, if they turned their backs and refused, Anathea would plague society as a whole and they'd be the cause of mass suffering. Naturally, no one wished this, and therefore did their "societal service".

To the populace, it was a noble thing to be punished for sin. Whipism kept their Order in check and it was right to persecute those who sought the Old World of "anarchy and gross wickedness". Indeed, many a time if one did wrong, they'd ask to be whipped or imprisoned. They felt that retribution for their transgressions absolved them from Anathea's anger and put them back in her good graces. It was an evil dogma: one that made people voluntarily hate themselves.

During the video, a ten year-old boy laughed to another kid and took Gabriel's name in vain. Unfortunately for him, the teacher heard and stopped the film. The little kid was asked to walk to the front of the class and hold his arms up for five minutes. For the first minute or so, he was utterly berated and scolded–essentially on trial.

The teacher then instructed the class to ask the boy questions; if he got them wrong, he'd be hit hard with a ruler on his arms. He was asked about six and got three wrong. By the end of it, he was in tears and Peter silently wept for the child. He did not make a peep for the rest of the period once he returned to his seat. Peter was furious with the teacher and dreamt of him being eternally whipped for having been so spiteful, unsympathetic, and mean.

As unbelievable as it seems, that was not nearly the darkest event at school that day.

Peter was to go to English next. While they sat waiting, the teacher brought in a recently killed pig that had been sacrificed. Offering animals to their goddess was seen as a good thing–that it brought her joy that they wanted the animals to "go to Heaven early".

Horrifyingly, the students were to take small cups and drink minute amounts of its blood. The fluid contained the "lifeforce" bestowed on living creatures and it would help *instill more life into the students so that they'd become honorable*. It disgusted Peter and Janet beyond comprehension and they only pretended to sip it. The dogma ran deep, and the people had no intention of escaping the abyss.

At the end of the day, an unforeseen assembly took place. Announced over the intercom, the students and staff made their way there without knowing the purpose. Once all upon the bleachers, the principal came in with an enraged face. He held up Janet's book and demanded the culprit(s) come forward. The two friends held each other's hands and grew very scared. They hoped there was no way of linking them to it and that no cameras saw them.

After about an hour of dead silence from the crowd and constant lectures by the principal, he threw the book in a metal bucket and burned it before the assembly. He declared that they'd all have to attend school over the weekend as punishment. He explained that anyone found with similar items would be handed over to the World Guards.

The World Guards indeed were to be feared. They were the one-world military of sorts, instructed to preserve the New World. They wore pure white armor, carried whips on the belts, and most held flamethrowers or high powered rifles. No one dared fight against them or backtalk.

Janet realized then just how stupid she was earlier. She swore to herself that she'd never risk doing such a thing again. If caught, she would likely be thrown in a re-education camp, or possibly worse…

CHAPTER 5

The Census

It would be two weeks later when a census was to take place in the city. An annual census ensured that the government could fully monitor the population and keep it in check. If there were too many humans, the Department of Breeding would have to either raise the standard of excellent genetic parental stock or refuse many who wished to have children. A ceiling on bearing personal children was already in place. Some who were of lesser stock–if allowed to breed–could only have one or two children. On the other hand, those of the highest, most precious superiority, could reproduce much more.

All were required to attend the censuses, regardless of age. People were generally very excited for them, as either Gabriel or his disciples would give speeches afterwards. Seeing as how Peter did not live in a major city, it was unlikely for Gabriel to be there in person.

Peter and his father ended up meeting with Janet and her parents on the way there. It was always fairly awkward when the two families were together. Janet's parents were strict followers of dogma; never could their god-fearing stomachs be sated. Although unsure, Peter suspected that they knew his father was unemployed. It was for that reason they looked down upon him. He figured Janet must've commented numerous times on him being home while she came over to be with Peter. At any rate, Peter's father abominated them more, but loved Janet dearly. Strange, that he likely knew Janet (her true self) more than even her own parents.

There was a greatly immense stadium in the heart of the city where large events and declarations were made. It was there that the census took place. Before making it there, the people stopped to watch a mass parade for the yearly event.

The partakers of it were almost solely World Guards and other military commanders. They'd march in beautiful, yet sinister order down the streets with their flamethrowers and rifles in hand. Very advanced and futuristic war vehicles, tanks, artillery, and surveillance technology, were shown off in droves as far as the eye could see.

The entire street and stadium was drenched and overshadowed in the colorful Anathean flags. A grand display of at least 40,000 in number must have been present over only a few miles. The flags were red–indicating the life-giving blood within everyone; a black lioness was upon it–symbolizing her fierce power over darkness; and a sharp, bloody sword was held between the animal's teeth–indicating her intense persecution over the godless.

To an Old-Worlder's ears, the loud music that played as they went by would sound spine-chilling and formidable. Music of the New-World was invented by the Aristocrats, so the people were raised thinking it was magical. The notes were always in an abnormal key, meter was off, and the frequencies were usually at 19 hz in order to subconsciously instill fear into the people's minds. They would have loud speakers blasting recordings of Gabriel reading passages from his book.

Again, the whole show of force was pointless. There were no other militaries nor countries to fight against. The danger was *terrorism*. They all lapped up the parade and mighty forces without realizing that it was, in truth, used to keep group-think and prevent them from having their own thoughts. The creation of the military as a whole was to not only kill, but utterly destroy someone like Peter–to burn him to ashes and annihilate the remnants. It was an ironic thing: those who opposed the military (called *terrorists*) were seen as dangerous; yet, the military and all their legal weapons of death were seen as protectors of peace. The so-called protectors of peace subdued those who were against their licenses to kill.

To expound on weapons, it should be fairly obvious why they were illegal. Originally, Gabriel quickly outlawed firearms so none could go against his Guards or attempt to displace him or his elites. As time went on and people got comfortable having none whatsoever (long knives, swords, bows, explosives of all kinds, fuels, toy guns, etc.), the people became even more compliant, knowing that they couldn't challenge anyone, regardless if they felt like it.

After the parade, they quickly shuffled to the entrance of the stadium. In front of it were large golden and silver statues of the dictator and his elites. They looked almost too fit, too beautiful, and too immaculate–almost like the sculptures of ideal men and women the ancient Greeks had carved.

And yet, the figures weren't entirely off. He and his elites possessed the highest and best medicines/machines of the day. Some slowed their aging greatly, while others prevented almost all diseases. Such cures were available only to them and the people were oblivious to their existence. The elites did not want them in the hands of the people, for they did not wish them to forever stay young. The most rebellious of all people are the youth–and it was they who were monitored and controlled most. Hence, Gabriel wanted youth to pass as quickly as possible. Meanwhile, he wanted the deaths of the elderly (at the time), who faintly remembered the Old-World, most. The dictator thought it better to harm them as much as possible, but without directly committing genocide on them. He felt his Order had been working without the need to do so, but the evil thought still dwelt in his mind. Thus, they would never be given good medical treatments but left to wither away in the nightmare that was their new lives–without say, without disobedience, without happiness.

Gabriel's held a stone tablet that read the most serious and precious laws of the world. Some read, "Praise Anathea at all times", "Accept your savior", and "Value your responsibilities". He wore three consecutive crowns, each upon another, symbolizing his three-fold nature: himself, his mother, and her spirit that descended unto him; the unholy trinity.

Each of the Aristocrats held menacing spears in one hand and ornate shields in the other: one for vanquishing evil, the other for protecting the Order. Of course, they would never be as venerated or revered as Gabriel, nor have such a tenacious grip, but they were nevertheless *lower lords* who held dominance over all facets of life. They were seen almost as Anathea's secondary children who gained her holy spirit as her chosen son had done before them. They were worshiped; they were feared; they were idolized.

Peter and the rest walked in a single-file line as they passed through the gate. One-by-one, they would hold up their wrists and the World Guards would scan their barcodes, instantly logging them into the census. As a gift for coming, they would then each be given bags filled with copious amounts of Rapts while they went inside to sit. It was a fantastic incentive to go anywhere; more so than even money of the Old World, for no money could provide as much pleasure as the happy capsules.

Upon entering the stadium, Peter saw what was unfortunately all too common. Thousands of cameras were planted throughout the dome in both expected and unexpected places. They were in plain sight, yet the people paid no mind. It was so customary, that they simply looked over them or didn't care.

Down below, in the center of the field, was an elaborate stage and podium, clad in red, black, and gold. Surrounding the whole structure was a highly-electrified, razor-wire steel fence with guards patrolling the perimeter. It wasn't needed, but it can be assumed they wanted to drill in the fact that they were "unconquerable".

While they all waited, there was a slideshow that played on an enormous holographic television attached to the ceiling. It showed people doing "good deeds" and following the ways of Anathea and their leader. Masses of people, dressed in black, would pray in front of statues of the goddess, while other scenes were of the faithful laughing and mocking the homeless as they passed by. Then there were hard workers in factories using heavy tools and machinery with smiles on their faces because they were progressing the Order. Peter and Janet's faces remained wry the whole time. The whole video looked almost *too cinematic* and not just caught on camera, as though possibly staged. There was no way to know.

It was shortly after that the speech began. Naturally, Gabriel wasn't there–instead having one of his Aristocrats to speak on his behalf. And yet, Gabriel did give a few words over the hologram. It was likely a recording he sent out to every city.

When the disciple (Arthur) stepped out, he was surrounded by other elites dressed in fine grey suits. They were businessmen-like and for the most part unknown. He began with a loud, flamboyant voice–much like Gabriel.

Now, it would be fairly useless to quote his speech, for the New Language was strong, and none of the Old World could properly understand it. It was, however, extremely elegant, well-versed, and refined. The people were entranced by it and fell silent. They stared with awe and glee, as though children listening to their favorite celebrity. As "beautifully" expressed as it was, it'd seem very frightful to those of the past.

Halfway through it, the people couldn't help but grin widely and cry tears of joy. They shouted afterwards: "Bless you!", "We are wretches, save us!", "Grace be unto the Order!", "Curse the protesting demons!, "Ego, freedom: revile!", "Death, damnation afflict the ungodly!". They were frenzied with intolerance and mad with their justice. It was all very surreal.

A line of slaves chained together by the feet then were led on stage. They each had a plaque strapped to their chest reading their crimes. Arthur then walked behind each one and explained why the Department of Breeding and group-think was inconceivably important. The slaves prevented illumination, enlightenment, and unity. They led the people astray from salvation. Illegal breeding produced *bad stock* raised by Anti-Anthea-ist parents.

There was great focus on one of the criminals who was considered the worst. He had reportedly attempted to assassinate one of Gabriel's disciples. He gave a long lecture about the man and his evildoings, until the darkest part of the whole event occurred. Arthur slowly and gently brought out a knife hidden under his robes and held it up. He pronounced that if the man believed that the messiah should not live, then the man–who was a demon–deserved his life to be taken from him a hundred times over. The people screamed with encouragement. "Glory, glory!", they cried. Then, in an instant, the Aristocrat thrusted the dagger into the man's heart.

"His heart was not focused on Anathea!" He yelled. "He slandered the name of Anathea's son and her children!"

Peter shook with fear and wanted to escape, but knew he couldn't. He shut his eyes tightly once he saw the wicked arm move. He was in the true devil's playground: eternally punished inside and ill with their diseases. He was metaphorically stabbed in his own heart and wept quietly for the man who very well may have been innocent.

The census concluded shortly afterwards with the man's body being dragged off stage. Arthur gave some closing arguments before the audience left. He demanded they continue to follow the rules, have faith in their leaders, and honor the New Age.

Peter grew sick as they slowly walked home. He felt like throwing up and crying at the same time, but knew he'd have to keep it in, lest others (Janet's parents specifically) noticed his disapproval. Janet remained completely silent, and Peter assumed she felt the same way. Peter was sensitive and Janet had a childish heart. She must've borne the brunt of grave sadness and empathy. They'd each take a handful of Rapts later that night.

Speaking of which, they resumed school the following day. Their first teacher handed out Rapts to all of the students the second she entered. It was a sick thing–especially given the fact that there were some children as young as twelve in the classroom. Indeed, it wasn't so much of a choice for the teachers to pass them out. No, it was mandated by the government. Yet, things were so deranged that the faculty would still do it out of their beliefs–regardless if required. To them, *they were making their students happy and more comfortable with learning; truly then, accordingly, how was she in the wrong?* So would say the parents.

The students were given an assignment to research and present an essay on "what is moral and why immorality harms society". A project of that nature would appear quite pleasant and helpful in normal circumstances. Morality of the Order was the opposite of orthodox beliefs. What was moral in the New Times could not be confounded with the old lessons of empathy, self-awareness, and altruism. *New morality* was thoughtlessness, insensitivity, subservience, and authoritativeness. They spat on anything of the old, even if it in some way matched their dogma.

Peter and Janet would research on one of the schools "hyper-computers". They functioned similarly to previous computers, but could compute the most difficult equations in under half a second. It had an AI software embedded within it that gave instant answers to almost any question. One was free to search anything they desired on them, but anything illegal was immediately censored and they'd be reported. They would be blocked out of the device in an instant and possibly flagged by the World Guards. It was therefore especially important that the two controlled their typing. Being a fairly minor offense (or so it would seem), the usual repercussions from the school would entail earning less Rapts per day. Because of severe dependence, people greatly feared being held back from their doses.

Janet's project would focus on the moral aspect of piety and its purpose. She would explain how the ultimate goal in life is to get on Anathea's good side, else they should become slaves indefinitely. She'd attempt to take their demented logic as far as it could go. People were not fixed-minded, you understand. In a sense, they were in terms of ideology, but Gabriel had the ability to constantly mold and reshape that ideology as much as he wanted. It was generally the case–as insane as it seems–that people who became and acted evermore crazed and obsessed with Anathea were perceived as divine and those to be emulated. If Janet cursed her neighbor or fellow classmate boy for not being *dedicated to the Order enough*, she could say so and the people would both honor her and condemn him. They were, in a sort, a society of children: bullying those who did not fit in and following the leader like baby pups.

It was a few days later when they were to present. The unease Peter felt as he stepped in front of the class and teacher cannot be understated. He feared accidentally saying an incorrect word and felt nothing less than dread. He was not an anxious boy, but to pronounce one's faux mind (and keep it in check) in front of a group of ravenous panthers was daunting. He knew very well that he needed to deeply think before speaking.

Indeed, he spoke well and thoroughly elaborated on his points, but the dead silence of the room and lack of expression from the teacher dismayed him. He had no knowing of whether he did good, so could only pray.

It was then Janet's turn. She started off "correctly", but as she continued, began to speak illegalish phrases and words, while not quite giving enough credit to their Order. Immediately, Peter's bowels quaked and his stomach entangled into a knot. He yearned for her to stop and grew deeply worried. She didn't seem to mean what she was talking about, but when one begins to adhere to something else so strongly (the truth), it's hard to keep up with all of the lies. She used only one or two Old World words and ideas, but it was more than enough. Perhaps it was actually out of spite that she did it, but more likely by accident. She'd never risk her livelihood over something so mundane. And still, the teacher was expressionless, showing neither approval nor disapproval. If he was angered, his wrath would come later.

After class, Janet was asked to stay after while Peter was packing away his things. He knew he wasn't pleased and she'd surely be punished. Standing up for her, he went up beside her and explained that he had edited the presentation for her. He told how he changed many of the words and accidentally slipped up. The teacher was vexed with him and lost all patience that such a scandal (as they would call it) occurred. He apologized profusely, but it changed nothing.

The teacher swiftly excused Janet and took Peter to the "Discipline Center" of the school. An old man sat at a desk with a sickening look upon his face. Only *unacceptable people* went to him. The teacher left him alone when the man played a recording of the presentation in front of them. The man's face reddened and he scowled at the boy.

"Do you think this is okay?" He asked angrily. "This is appropriate to you?"

He continually berated Peter for the next hour–harsh words after even harsher words. The man was offended by him and his illegal speech. A person like him was repulsed by such a conspicuous show of misbehavior. Meanwhile, humble Peter said nothing but looked down at the floor with his head down. The man got on the phone and contacted someone who would lower his social credit score. Peter would have to be without Rapts for the next three days. Although knowing it was a good thing, it killed him knowing the side-effects of withdrawals.

The next days were as he expected. Withdrawals from Rapts were beyond excruciating; more so than any other drug. The extreme addictive effects of them were intended by the government, and the dependence was scathing. No one got off of them at their own free-will. He'd have headaches, bone aches, obsessive itchiness, extreme nausea, bad hallucinations, and near-psychosis. It was a terrible thing. He'd lay in bed, desiring reprieving sleep, but could not. It got to the point that he longed for death–as though he had the worst possible illness without relief or minor remedy.

After awhile, he had at last gotten over it and felt well. Soberness was a new sensation to him. He'd been under influence for so long that he had forgotten what it was like to be normal. It felt nice, but even the happiest person could not be as elated as when under Rapts. For the first time, he thought he was his true self. He promised he'd never get back on the horrid drugs.

CHAPTER 6

Finding The *Others*

The next three weeks had been eating Peter's innards away. He had been working progressively harder for the Department of News without much leisure time.

He stood by his office window one morning. He saw the two opposing parts of the city: the High-Side and the Low-Side; it was in the likeness of the Community Pantries; for the world was split between those with the most fidelity and faith. It was a form of natural classism, where men naturally build hierarchy, though everyone was supposedly equal. All were provided with basic necessities free of charge, but those with the highest, prized and glorious credit had more wherewithal and means. Hence, all strived to be the best, most *unerring* people they could. As it was, it wasn't even out of greed or selfishness. They felt, as it were, that it was proper to be rewarded more for their level of religious adherence. The same was true of drugs and of course, food.

Even having been an internship, his society wanted to milk people for as much as they could and as long as possible. Because of how economics works–that everything was free–people had to work 'til death, endlessly producing goods that the government mandated them to.

He was in charge of full-time writing articles about that time. Generally, they would rebuke supposed criminals and admonish the people concerning them. Most had smuggled weapons, books, Old Word newspaper/texts, film, and music. The pieces would always end with: *"And so they were burned for their actions against order and peace"*. His work was very slimy, as one could call it. He'd write article after article, each under a different fake name, so as to give the impression that there were infinitely more people like him who believed the same things. He'd drill into the minds of people the horrors, disruptions, and ungodly actions of the illegals; constantly warning the people of the consequences.

He'd drink in constant shame while writing them, knowing he was doing wrong. By the end of each day, he was properly drunk. The alcohol, although helping, could not fully ease his mind knowing the immorality and unprincipled words he created and propagated. His social credit had been rising exponentially for the time being, and as much as he wanted to quit, he simply could not bring himself to do it. The temptations were too strong.

Because of his increased credit, he had the ability to live in the moderately-High-Side. As tempted as he was and desired a better life, he wanted to remain humble and continue to stay with his father in their lifelong homestead. Even if he lost interest in his childhood home that reminded him of his mother, he wanted nothing to do with being neighbors who were fanatics and overzealous. Anxiety would ramp up a hundred-fold with the dogmatic diehards who watched as lions, guarding their precious holy district.

After a good while of doing this, his boss approached him one day. Satisfied with his work, he declared Peter's new job would be a propaganda specialist. This time, it was an official job, and he could not decline.

The position angered Peter even more and his heart sunk with heavier weights. He'd have to design posters, write television scripts, and assist authors with writing Anathean books thereon. As well, he'd have to manage continuing creating articles. It has a tough load, but he knew he'd manage it. It was after that, that his credit skyrocketed. It sweetened his work, but wasn't nearly enough to convert him to their disgusting ways.

One day, he was asked to go to Hethers Hall in another larger city the next night. He wasn't told what for, but had a bad feeling about it. He assumed he'd interview someone or report on religious terrorists. Knowing the news, however, anything was possible.

He made his way to the Hall before nightfall. The city was different from his own, but had the same rules and beliefs—of course. For whatever reason, the bigger cities seemed more dystopian. One may conjecture that, since the population densities were equally bigger, control had to be tighter. This was likely to prevent substantial rebellions. As difficult as it is to believe, people there were even less sound. They fed off their dogma like a hyena feeds off of the most rancid meat. They prowled the streets, their eyes keen, always on the lookout for unholy beings to pounce on. They were places of even more paranoia, and criminals avoided them as much as possible.

Upon approaching the building, he found it completely closed off from the public. Razor-wire fences with black wooden sheets attached to it surrounded the perimeter, save one small gate with a security guard. When told that Peter was acting as a reporter, the man asked to scan his wrist. The barcodes showed everything about a person: their criminal record, birthdate, credit score, occupation, clearances, etc. Finding him truthful, he let him in.

He was therein met by another man who said he'd been waiting for him for awhile. When asked what exactly the job was, the man said nothing except: "take good pictures" and "do your best". Obviously, Peter was quite confused and thought it strange that everything seemed quiet. He was not filming a riot or anything of that sort.

The man pulled him back to something like a film setup. He was utterly shocked at what he was seeing. It was in front of the steps of the building. A large statue of Anathea stood there. A man with a sledgehammer in his hand pretended to hit the statue with a furious face. Around this, were staged fires that looked unnatural, but were purposefully put there. Another man then stepped out. His shirt was off, skin and face dirty, and held a large machine gun in his hand.

"3, 2, 1…" Yelled a seemingly director.

The man held the gun high in the air and pretended to scream with pure hatred.

"Go Peter! Hurry." Said the director.

Peter then knelt down and snapped dozens of photographs. Afterwards, the men stepped away and smiled, for they did a "good" job. Peter felt nauseous at that moment. He knew precisely what was taking place. The whole "riot" was staged, made up, and a lie. He already distrusted the department, but he realized anything and everything he wrote about may have been done by the same people in the same fashion. He no longer knew what was real.

"Well done, kid." The director said. "Those are some beautiful pics and the department will be happy."

Peter's disposition was a mix between sadness, depression, and glum. He slowly made his way back home. As he sat on the hyper-train, he popped three pills of Rapts in his mouth, trying to numb the feelings of villainous fraudulence. He felt no sense of honor nor dignity, and thought he didn't deserve it. He accepted that Janet was right all along and he should never have accepted the internship. He was trapped and could never go back to his normal life of being a small outcast in society. Even if he willingly did his job badly from then on, he could get demoted, but never fired. He was simply stuck.

Perhaps as expected, Peter's boss was impressed at his work and instructed him to then write an article about the "terror" at Hethers Hall. He was to say they vandalized a sanctuary and attempted to initiate a revolt. His pictures would be on the main headlines of every one.

Peter couldn't help but be cross. He solemnly questioned his boss, but was taken as talking back. Peter professed how he knew the story was fake and disagreed with publishing it. Of course, that did not go well. His superior immediately lashed out at him, demanding that he did what he was told without question. Peter apologized quickly, knowing there was no use arguing and that it'd only end terribly. He did, in fact, write them. He knew his ethos was destroyed and hated himself for it.

The thought continued to persist in his mind of how his life would graduate if he only gave in morally to their standards and willingly tried to succeed in their expectations. He already faked a smile, but to completely alter his outward appearance, simply to heighten his social standings, was inconceivable. Peter still knew not who he fully was and didn't know his place moreso, but would never lower his ethos for such a dark precept as Anathea, let alone even humoring the dictator.

A few nights later, Janet unexpectedly showed up to Peter's house. She felt lonely and needed to confide in him. The first thing Peter noticed was a fairly nasty burn on her right hand. When asked what happened, he related how she was caught saying illegal words and terms with another student. The teacher (who brought in the pig before), forced her to hold her hand over a candle for thirty seconds as punishment. Peter was understandably angry.

Although she was in great pain, she was more thankful that they didn't lower her credit, which would've taken away her Rapts privileges. It was her first official offense, so the repercussions were not as harsh as they could have been. She said how she felt the teacher was "out to get her", for some reason, but didn't know why. Peter thought it may have had something to do with failing her tests and purposely not answering basic questions correctly. A question like: "Which option is the best course of action when finding an Old Worlder?". She'd answer with an blatantly incorrect option of: "Try having a conversation with them". The one they were looking for was: "Report them at once".

She said the reason for coming over was to convince him of going with her to the mysterious shack. It was late, but the only time possible to go, and she didn't want to be alone. Besides, Peter wanted to see it for himself. At first, he was reluctant to venture so far away with the possibility of getting caught. Yet, he couldn't refuse the opportunity to find old treasures. There was only so much he could learn from his meager collection and he needed more to satisfy his yearning for knowledge.

It may have been impossible for the two to go–even at night–if it weren't for "stealth packs". It was an illegal personal piece of technology that let someone hide from cameras and surveillance technology. It didn't make a person invisible, but shrouded them from electronic eyes. It created something like a magnetic shield around them and scrambled signals.

It wasn't particularly against the law to sneak out of the city when not taking the proper roads/rails. If caught, however, it was certain for that person to be put on the government's radar.

They'd be watched and monitored far more than they already were. If tracked or flagged, the two friends could likely not go again, at the risk they were followed the second time.

Despite this, there was a mandatory curfew throughout the city. This was to discourage private assemblies that would often take place under the cloak of nighttime. This made the stealth packs even more important.

Once Peter agreed, they packed up lightly and left swiftly. The supposed shack was up a nearby mountain, and that may have contributed to it not having been discovered. As they trekked up, Peter saw the glow of lights in the distance from the slave camps. He recalled his uncle being taken there years ago for refusing to work, and hadn't seen him since. He didn't know what went on in the camps, only that they were worse than prisons. The fact that they had "re-education" in their name suggested that the slaves were gravely changed or molded in some way.

"Rehabilitation" in Anathean society was far more effective than one of the Old World would expect. Peter did know that the government had state-of-the-art lie detectors–ones almost impossible to beat. He figured they utilized them in the camps, but there was no way of knowing. If true, and he were in their shoes, he'd never be freed.

They approached the break in the city fences and climbed through. By this time, they were in the middle of nowhere in the woods at night. All Peter could rely on was his flashlight and Janet's directions. About 10 minutes later, their lights moved on the old shack in the distance.

When they opened it, Peter was amazed just how strange it was. Most homes in the city were in bad shape and dilapidated, but the shack seemed different. It too, was in the same condition, but many of the objects in it were outdated and out of time. This was corroborated by the thick layer of dust spread evenly over the counters.

He couldn't tell if the things were from the Old World, or just early New World. There were old bottles of alcohol in a cabinet. They had brand labels on them, unlike ones produced by the government. They may've been illegal and Peter didn't want to risk taking some. Although old, many of the things were broken, destroyed, or torn apart, so there wasn't reason to get excited. It seemed as though the place was already found and half-way demolished; perhaps even ransacked.

As they searched up and down, Peter found a picture frame underneath a chair. The picture in it showed a family. They must've been from the 2010s at the latest. A father, a mother, three children. They were dressed nicely, smiled, and looked happy. It made Peter sad, knowing families like that used to exist. Save his elderly father, Peter had none. He couldn't imagine if something ever happened to him or Janet.

As they continued going about, they all of the sudden heard a thud coming beneath the floorboards, as though something had fallen. At first, they thought they must have misheard, as the small shack was only one story and without a basement.

Janet then asked for Peter's help moving a couch over. Like before, she inferred it would be a good place to find a secret book. It was then, to their surprise, that they found a wooden trap door beneath it. Letting curiosity get the best of them, they opened it to discover a dark, deep, cold tunnel that ran under it.

Peter was eager to follow it but Janet stopped him. She said how it could lead to anywhere: maybe a secret military base, or something worse. She didn't like the fact, knowing that something moved down there without saying a word. Peter mollified her, though, convincing her that such mysteries are the reason for coming there–to find truths.

Hesitantly, the two hopped down and slowly shuffled down the tunnel, praying their lights didn't go out. After about five or so minutes, they came to the end, where they found a metal door carved into the compact dirt. There was a painted symbol on the door: a white, opened hand with a red candle in its palm. Noises seemed to come from the other side of it, so

Peter put his ear against it. They sounded like faint whispers or voices. It was difficult to make out, but they did not sound like World Guards. No, these people were purposefully trying not to be found.

In a moment of intrigue, Peter knocked on the door. Janet grabbed onto his arm, angry that he was acting so bold. Immediately, the voices ceased and all became quiet. Then, after a scary pause lasting for what seemed like a lifetime, someone uttered something.

"What's the password?" Said someone on the other side.

Peter asked who they were and the purpose of their hiding, but the man would not budge. Peter deduced that, since they were normal people, the only reason they'd be keeping quiet was because they were criminals. In a daring attempt that could've costed them their lives, Peter said he agreed with them and were searching for banned items. The voices from the otherside began to speak again, as if they were considering Peter among themselves.

Peter immediately regretted it and thought he'd gotten too courageous. They just admitted that they were Anti-Anathea-ists.

It was then, however, that the tumblers on the door moved and it opened slightly. A boy's face looked at them and asked if they found anything and why they were searching for old paraphernalia. Peter replied that they wanted to learn about history and the *elder ways*.

The boy smiled and let them in, apparently full of trust.

Once entered, they found a room like no other seen before. It was filled to the brim with every illegal object unknown to man. There were televisions, full bookshelves, weapons, posters, old food, old clothing, maps, toys/gadgets, medicines, and so much more. If they were ever caught, there was a good chance they'd be killed on the spot. It was for that reason, that it was all the more shocking they let the two in.

There were three rebels in the bunker. The first boy, who's name was apparently "Knox" was about to talk to them when another girl interrupted and told them to leave.

"You knew the symbol?" Asked Knox to Peter and Janet.

"Symbol?" Said Peter.

"So, you just so happened to find this place?" He said. "The hand and candle represents those of the light holding a candle of enlightenment. It is widely use amongst the rebels to identify their meeting places."

The group seemed to ease up and Knox introduced themselves. He and a girl named "Arra" were the youngest, being only 22 years-old. The other man, "Zempher", was fairly old in his mid-sixties. He was by far the wisest out of all of them and remembered the Old World in depth.

They relayed their whole life stories to the two, after Peter and Janet explained themselves.

Apparently, Zempher had been a slave a few years prior for being caught with a mysterious "Bible". It was then that he met Knox, who worked part-time as a security officer in the camp from the age of 16 until present. They befriended each other, knowing that both believed in the same creeds.

Knox was, for the most part, a slacker in school, but a savant of mechanics. He was the one who found the old doomsday bunker and refurbished it.

Once Zempher was freed, he remained poor and homeless on the streets; ex-slaves lose all housing privileges for life. It was then that Arra was walking along at dusk and stopped to give him *wealthy* food she'd snuck out of the DFS factory. They too, became companions, and it was through him that she was introduced to Knox. Because his social credit score was destroyed and he was unable to get daily rations of all things and sustain himself, Zempher had been staying with Knox ever since.

Meanwhile, Arra worked part-time in the Division of Food Security (DFS). They were the lead factories that would produce the country's food. She had light brown hair, bright green eyes, and appeared very innocent or kind-hearted.

Before losing his entitlements, Zempher worked in the language sector: The Center of Proper Language Use, or CPLU. One would think it strange working while being so old, but retirement was abolished many moons ago. The CPLU was only slightly less dangerous than the Department of News, but equal in the level of government turpitude and tyranny. It was an institution of language management; and truly, he who controls what can and cannot be said, controls thoughts and actions across the board.

Zempher's job was erasing history, though they called it, *"setting the record straight"*. He aided higher-ups with locating unacceptable books and instructing the Guards where they could find and destroy them. He'd also come up with ideas to falsify the past in New World books. Peter was somewhat familiar with the latter, composing lies himself in his articles. It killed Zempher far more, so he was thankful for being jobless–as terrible as that was.

Peter and Janet stayed with them for the next few hours and discussed the beauties of the old ways, as well as how sick their situations were. They all had this idea that they were somehow born with a different spirit, unlike the rest. That lies and malevolence didn't affect them. If that was true, they knew there'd be more like them in the wild, hiding, just as they were.

Both Peter and Janet's hearts were warmed for those hours and they felt elated that there were others like them thinking the same things. They always thought they were alone in the world–fighting a losing battle against the great evil.

The two knew they'd have to leave soon, as sunrise was approaching. They weren't granted as much time to fully get to know the other rebels but knew they'd come across their paths again–especially now they had their own little headquarters. Before saying farewell, Knox gave the two the passcode to get in whenever they felt like it. It was a kind gesture that they trusted Peter and Janet enough after such little time, but no Anathean could possibly pretend to be a rebel, for it was the worst and most wicked thing they could do, knowing the goddess was watching. They were told to remember the code and never disclose it; not even under the threat of death. Truly, if one did, they would all suffer the flamethrowers.

As they descended the mountain, a heavy bout of snow began falling. Winter was quickly approaching and the two knew what that meant. Winter was the most devastating time of year and they'd have to switch their mindsets from depression to survival.

CHAPTER 7

Arra's Sickness

Arra sat on the hyper-train, waiting patiently to arrive at the Division of Food Security. The hyper, hover trains moved at subsonic speeds slightly off the ground. They were always ghostly, as the people–all in the same dress–usually didn't say anything and sat silently with a small grin upon their faces. Perhaps they were in a constant state of contemplation, or they simply didn't wish to accidentally offend anyone: a common mode of action. To elaborate briefly, offensive speech was just as antipathetical as using incorrect, established language. There was the idea of *ego violence*; the fact that selfishness, "lack of empathy", or even words could be violent to one's psyche/emotions. It was extremely dark, but not often observed.

As the trains were so fast and the distance was short, she got to the plant in under fifteen minutes. The plant was a disgusting place. Due to the lack of resources in an economic egalitarian society, like that of Communism, the plant processed the worst of food. They grew bugs for consumption that they'd make into drinks or bars, and refined moldy/rotten edible plants and their fruits to make them safe to eat. As bad as that seemed, the worst part was that they were added to baby food/formulas, whence would be sent to the Department of Breeding.

Many children would be forced to work in the factories when out of school to aid the labor force–some as young as four. They were generally the students who performed badly or did not meet the highest standards. The latter students would often be offered jobs in intelligence jobs, such as the one Peter had.

Horribly, many of the children (and even adults), would be hit with little whips if they did not meet quality expectations; as though ten year-olds could accomplish such a thing. Arra would often hear their little cries and wept for them, many a time crying and tearing up. She dreamed of beating the Guards up, and giving them endless lashes, sometimes even killing them for their terrible deeds. They were the scum of the Earth for what they did.

Children were not as valued in the Anathean world as much as teenagers or adults. They were seen as the most unrestrained and free-thinkers in society. They would need strict discipline to become worthy and God-fearing citizens. The same was obviously true with the oldest people.

Arra was disgusted and exceedingly angry about all of it. She would frequently vomit on her breaks and sob. She repeatedly had major depressive episodes where she didn't wish to leave bed and refuse work, but again, she had no choice. Her life would become even worse if she merely skipped days. Her rations would lower, her drugs would cease to be, and she would be in a worse state than she already was. Her only reprieves were Rapts and constant drunkenness. Like all of her friends, Peter, and Janet, she desired escape, but it was simply impossible.

A good question may be why robots didn't handle jobs. The technological society was certainly capable of it. Yet, if so, the people would not work, and this was entirely against the will of Anathea and would mean no one contributed to her holy creation of making humans slaves. Just as well, it would make people *cancers*, sustaining and feeding off her "plentiful Earth", with giving her nothing in return. To them, she saw work as a form of sacrifice–that the harder they labored to take care of one another, the higher the chances of afterlife rapture.

At the same time, Peter was on his way to work. As he walked in the cold rain, he passed by the lines of homeless people lying on the sidewalks. Many of them had large bruises, lash marks, or bloody cuts. There was a World Guard carelessly throwing drugs at them to keep them quiet and happy. They begged Peter for food and water. He desperately wanted to give them some, but he had none on his person. Regardless, the Guards and cameras were watching and it was a highly discouraged thing to do to help them; not illegal, but an advisement against.

He'd frequently stop to provide them with company, as it was natural for ex-slaves and prisoners to be shunned from the public for the rest of their lives, regardless if they were "rehabilitated" exceptionally. Even "freed" and dwelling amongst each other with equal experiences, they were lonely and still fought amongst each other for food. Starving and desperate animals would also come upon them, attack, and attempt to steal the little they already had.

Peter was free of Rapts, and he swore he'd never get on them again. However, he passed the outlet and the temptation for elation and unrestrained pleasure made him stop. He decided to walk away but again turned around. His credit was high, and he could get more than he needed: more than necessary to get his daily fix. He clenched his teeth for a moment, knowing he couldn't resist. He held his face down with shame as he slowly walked over to get a couple. The provider of them looked more than joyous every time he handed them out. They tried to get all giddy-like and cheer Peter up, but his face could not lift an inch. He knew he was giving into the allure of numbness and a false sense of contentment. He popped a pill in disappointment.

He was swiftly told to have a meeting with his bosses the second he walked in the door. He became very scared, knowing he likely broke the rules in some fashion. Like when he started the job, they led him into a room, deathly silent, and sat him down with cold stares directed towards him. They brought out an article of his and pointed to the word "religion", used in the context of Anathean-ism.

He was reprimanded considerably for using it. Anathea-ism was *absolutely not* a religion, according to them. No, it was an undeniable truth. Unlike religion, there were no alternatives nor non-adherents. To question Anathea-ism was to question the government itself, thereby questioning Gabiel and the Department. It was so absurd to deny her, that to disbelieve in Anathea was to disbelieve basic truths that humans were living beings. He was not allowed to use the ancient word.

Why is free speech important? One may say because it makes people feel unrestrained. Another may conjecture that it makes all people feel included. They're both mistaken. Truth cannot thrive–let alone survive–without it. To speak freely is to speak what others don't wish to hear. It has almost always been the case that those people/ideas which one is not allowed to criticize are those who should be denounced. Expressing thoughts freely ensures that there is no one-and-only group-thought. To speak, is to give options and opinions; to not give an opinion, is to devoid the world of individuality; to remove the sense of the individual, is to create a tyranny of mere rote robotic people who follow only the only one-opinion–which can easily become or likely is a falsehood.

Peter had no right to his opinion, and therefore had no ability to change anything. In honesty, he didn't pay much mind to the backlash. He knew he was right and couldn't be persuaded otherwise. The worst that would happen was a demotion, yet he'd still have fine credit. They did indeed threaten him with it.

Oddly, Peter agreed with them and said he should have been punished for being so careless and inconsiderate. He knew that they'd probably do such a thing, but he'd remain in their good graces. They thought for a moment before deciding to sentencing him to one day in HR management without lowering his status. It would later be a good decision by repenting, as he did gain back their favor.

Human resources of the Old World went by a different name. It was called re-education training (of course), and was not fun. When Peter got to the head of it–a woman named Lilia–he was sat down and forced to watch a film. It was an hour-long compilation of inspirational speeches by Gabriel and his top followers. The videos depicted him talking about how upright the Order was, how it should be kept that we, lest chaos and eternal damnation befalls the people.

She then switched off the television, sat in front of him, and sporadically asked him questions while lecturing. Firstly, she asked whether he thought Anathea-ism was just a religion. Naturally, he answered no and rebutted with his assertion that she was his only true mother that would never be denied in his mind. The woman smiles, agreeing and saying just how disgusting it would be if he did think it as nothing more than a subjective belief. When asked why he used the word, he quickly had to make up an excuse. It took him a minute and minor beads of sweat formed on his forehead. He played it off as acting humiliated for doing it. He told her he was quoting some rebels and accidently got the words mixed up. It was a terrible excuse, hardly to be believed, but it was all he could come up with. She didn't enjoy the answer, but was properly fooled into thinking he was sorry, so she let it go. At the end, before leaving, she threatened him, saying how he'd be monitored more following the incident and he would not like to humor the consequences of a second offense.

For the remainder of the day, he was given an assignment to go to the Department of Breeding to take another set of pictures. He immediately had a sick feeling in his gut and knew it'd be similar to the Hethers Hall incident. The bosses always gave the instructions very vaguely. "Go to the Department. You'll meet someone there.", they'd say.

It was only about three miles away, so he decided to walk. He had never been in the breeding buildings and was quite hesitant, not knowing if scenes of horrors awaited him. Once taken back to the "processing center" by a man in a black lab coat, he saw the endless lines of babies being manhandled by workers examining, washing, and clothing them. The thunderous spew of cries rumbled the room and it was difficult to hear. Although natural for a baby to cry at every hour, it all seemed abnormal. Perhaps it was the way they were carelessly tossing the babies about, or simply the environment. Rather than resting upon their mothers' bossoms, they were in a rowdy foreign place, far removed from tender love and peace.

They walked by them until they entered the back rooms where the babies were immediately born before processing. There was a man and a woman waiting for Peter. The man was very tall and muscular, had fine hair, and essentially looked as though he had the ideal physique. Besides the muscles, the woman looked just as beautiful: almost like a princess taken straight out of a fairytale. They held their baby in their arms, wrapped in a wool blanket.

Peter was instructed to take a picture of them as they posed. This was not how the ordeal of births happened. In truth, once born, the baby would be taken to the processors. They would then move onto the *inspectors*, who'd decide if the baby was worthy of living. If not, one can imagine their fate. It'd only be after an arduous procedure that the family would see them again, ready for raising.

The next day, Peter would have to make and print posters of the picture, encouraging those with the perfect genes to bear fruit. The posters would then be hung in the streets, in buildings (including schools and hospitals), and advertised on the major television screens.

Feeling upset by all that he was doing, Peter decided to visit the bunker once again at night before curfew. He chose to go alone that time, wanting solitude from the talkative madness about him.

He stood outside his home before leaving, leaning against a wall to smoke a cigarette. He heard a small scream not three-hundred feet away and saw an old woman being knocked to the ground by a Guard. He chose to stay put, knowing it wouldn't work out good if he went over, but the feeling of anger took hold of him and forced his feet to move.

He rushed to her aid and demanded the man stop. In the same moment, Peter grabbed his arm to move the rifle barrel from the torso of the woman; it was an extremely foolish and stupid thing to do, but it was the right thing.

The Guard swiftly punched him in his gut and he fell to the ground.

"Leave, now!" The Guard yelled sternly. "Mind your business!"

Peter thought it was best to finally slowly limp away then, until the Guard changed him mind and instructed him to return.

"Better yet," he said, "why don't you take care of it. Lay a hit on her; perhaps it'll teach you a lesson about who belongs and who ought to be dealt with. You are on our side, correct?"

Obviously, Peter refused, until the Guard drew his pistol and pointed it at him.

"Do it!" He commanded. "Prove you're not going against the Guards' wills. You wouldn't want to give off that impression, would you?"

Peter had no choice; he had to comply, lest he be punished far worse than her. He walked up slowly and saw on her face an even glimpse of sympathy for the boy, knowing he didn't want to do it. He apologized and lightly punched her in her arm with as little force as he could, yet making it seem hard.

"Good." Said the Guard. "Now leave unless you want to be like her."

One could only guess the "crime(s)" she committed. She likely did nothing wrong at all and he was just having some violent "fun" with her to satisfy his sociopathic tendencies. He got to the bunker shortly thereafter.

He found himself alone there, which he thought was odd. He assumed the others came each night, but their duties and schooling must have taken much of their time–the same way as it did with him.

He roamed around the strange room, observing and analyzing all of the forbidden, exotic items. The amount of them was astonishing and because of that, he'd almost certainly be burned to death on the spot, were he caught with them.

He opened a box and discovered a plethora of Old World dehydrated food. Food in his society had almost no labels, save the name of the department it was manufactured in and the type of food–similar to an MRE. These, on the other hand, had a million different words and pictures. What surprised him most was a "nutritional information" spread sheet on the back of it. No one except workers knew what was in their foodstuffs. Their trust was in their government that they were healthy and sustainable.

He decided to open one and try it. It was garlic and cheese pasta. He knew neither what cheese nor pasta was, so was quite eager. After adding hot water and waiting a few moments, he put a scoop in his mouth. His eyes instantly opened, taste buds screamed, and a wave of dopamine rushed through his brain. To an Old Worlder, such a dish was a quick and inexpensive meal not highly valued, but he'd never experienced such a beautiful flavor, so freshly prepared (despite being decades old). He scarfed it down as fast as he could, hypnotized by the savor of non-native taste. He had read fairly boring and uninformative outlawed books, but something as relishing as that really made him think about just how special and grand the before times really were.

He then walked about again, looking for another foreign enigma. He saw a pair of jeans and a t-shirt behind some boxes. He knew neither what they were nor called, only that they were clothes.

He put them on and was intrigued. They made him feel like a different person somehow, though not knowing who could have worn such fashion in the olden times.

Directly after, he went to the bookshelf and gandered at it. In the Old World, they were extremely prized books. Many were religious, philosophical, and popular works of fiction. Apparently, the rebels must've known they were quite important–likely because of Zempher. He pulled some out that were large and had only one to two word titles. The first was something called the "Bible", next was "Quran", and the third was "Vedas". He could hardly understand the Bible because of its very archaic words, but tried his best. The Quran was the same way. He read the first "Chapter" of each one and was utterly dumbfounded. They each gave a vastly different account of different gods, the world's creation, and the purpose of humanity. It took him hours re-reading even the first page of one of them simply to fathom such an odd way of thinking. Long in days past, he wouldn't know just how powerful and divided such manuscripts were. He would have no idea how almost all of the world's population believed in one of those three books.

Peter would return almost every night following the discovery. He'd expand his mind with other works by mysterious authors such as: Aristotle, Plato, Shakespear, Confucius, and Voltaire. Most of the words seemed to be in an alien language, but it did not dissuade him. He tried to deduce their meanings and became fairly successful at doing so. Somehow, in the back of his mind, he appreciated the language and thought that it was *freer*, but he couldn't explain why.

They seemed more meaningful, less constricted and bound. Each author said vastly different ideas without any amount of controlled thoughts.

A sentence came up in a book by Thomas Paine: *"It is the duty of every man, as far as his ability extends, to detect and expose delusion and error"*. He gazed at the sentence for roughly fifteen minutes, gulping up the words and digesting them. It made him consider how people saw tyranny in pre-Anathean times; that his neighbors were "delusional" in their thoughts; perhaps Anathea herself was merely a figment of imagination and the gods of other works could have more credence. He didn't know, but the quote impacted him in a way that cannot be described. It was talking to him: explaining that he had a sort of duty to release people from their thought-prisons. Very weird indeed.

He knew the books were religious and, by virtue of language, were exceedingly ancient. He wondered if people could survive without religion. Perhaps snippets here and there, but that most people need them; maybe for hope, faith, order, purpose, or security. He didn't know.

CHAPTER 8

The Question of Freedom

Of the many nights he had frequented the hideout in the shack, one was on a peculiar note. He was given a drug called LSD from a person trading drugs with him in the city. The trader simply told him it'd make him hallucinate. He was never adept, let alone acquainted with such a drug, so was interested to try it alone in a confined space where his nerves were calm and he needed not be paranoid of anything.

Drugs often made music sound sweeter, so he turned on a classical piece from Mozart which he'd never hearkened to. He grabbed the tab and held it to his mouth, anxious about the strength and how it would affect him. He finally let it dissolve on his tongue, laid back with his eyes closed and listened to the hypnotic, tranquilizing sounds of the record player.

He gently drifted off to sleep, and while another piece began to play, he found himself seeing funny shapes and auras. As he cried listening to the beautiful orchestra, he played a romantic film from the 1980s. In an instant, he felt transported into the movie, not seeing or experiencing the real, outside world. He was walking in a park, with clear skies, humble trees, and a light wind blowing the colorful flowers about: not wilted and dead from thick smog. Around him, he saw happy couples holding hands and smiling. There were children around them, chasing each other and laughing with Old World, unique clothes. They didn't have barcodes on their wrists; no one did. There were others sitting quietly and reading strange books on benches along the walkways.

The sense Peter experienced was like something he'd never felt. None of the people were starving, fearful, addicted to drugs, or mad. They were all equal and free to speak as they wished and moved without consequences. He couldn't help but sob watching the prettiness of it all.

Suddenly, once Peter blinked, he was in another setting. He was sitting in a chair of what smelled like a coffee shop. Looking around, he saw friends and families sitting together at other tables. They were laughing, eating healthy Old World food, and could freely order whatever they desired. He was amazed that only creative art belonged on the walls–not propaganda or dark posters. Most of all, Gabriel and Anathea were nowhere in sight; not even the faintest glimpse.

Again, he blinked, and Janet appeared in front of him holding a warm cup of colorful coffee. They didn't seem like friends, nor did he feel like they were anymore. They seemed utterly in love and yet again, Peter cried, but she didn't seem to notice. She wore clothes that were full of color and brightness. They were unearthly and caught his eyes something fierce. Peter wore a jacket and jeans, but didn't know what they were called. None of them were peasant clothes, but things that only Aristocrats could wear, if they chose to.

Peter then realized he was imagining all of it, and while seeing it, used his real eyes to grab a pen and paper. He tried to copy and draw the art on the walls, seeing them as attractive and important. He altered it a little–for the first time using his imagination. He put his own twist and style into it. Then, as quickly as it came, his knees broke beneath him, he fell, and his eyes shut.

He was awoken, sober, by the sound of people opening the door. It was Janet and Knox. They questioned what he was doing on the floor until they found the piece of paper in his hands. Their dispositions changed to wonderment and they were fascinated by the art. Things of that nature were not permitted and seen as heresy. People were not supposed to think as individuals and manifest their own "wills" that would be art.

Peter only vaguely remembered all that went on in the last hours but knew the sketch meant something meaningful. He simply lied to them, saying it came to him in a dream, when he knew it was under the influence. He decided to fold it and place it in his pocket to look at in the future, should he need inspiration.

They talked together for a few hours, discussing other places they could potentially scavenge for other items, but they debated whether they truly needed to. Their insatiability for novel things of the past, plus their already gluttonous selves of what they already possessed was strong, but the risks were evermore outweighing the rewards. The books and films especially, they could learn what may well have been infinite knowledge without any other materials.

Arra came later in the early morning. She brought up something that had dawned on her the previous day and was eager to get it off of her chest to the rest. She told how, as a kid, her mother relayed a story to her about a mysterious uninhabited island not far off the coast. She said how, (at least) at the time, it was free of the Order and completely unknown. Arra's grandfather often traveled there, being a sailor and seasoned seaman, for its beauty and seclusion.

Arra had dreamt of escaping there, starting a new life for her own, and liberating herself from the dogmatic dystopia her whole life. Yet, she never wanted to do it alone. Life would be pointless without anyone to interact with. She'd forgotten about the dream and unknown island as she grew, but the thought popped back into her mind and she longed for it more than ever.

The group knew what she was implying. She proposed that all of them flee to it. As said before, was the risk worth the reward? The idea resonated in all of them and knew it was a good idea. They were putting their lives on a pedestal for being seen and caught if they did such a thing. The risk was indeed extraordinary.

Regardless, Arra didn't know the coordinates–only the general direction of where it'd lie and they had no means of transportation to make it. If they agreed, they'd have to go all in, not turn back, plan, and work cautionally.

Arra mentioned that before making a decision, she'd talk to Zempher. At his age, they could only guess if he'd make the trip safely. He was their longtime friend and leaving him behind was out of the question. Heck, she thought, maybe he'd know where it was.

Before leaving, Knox told the group he had a present for them in celebration of Light Day. They obviously did not agree with the iniquitous holiday, but after learning about another one, he saw people used to give one another gifts. He brought out an old Iphone that he redesigned and refurbished. They had no clue what it was or did per se; just that it was a form of personal computer. Such things had long been banned for people had the potential to create "mis- and disinformation" on them which would "disrupt progress and spread hatred".

Of course, there was no internet nor data on it, but he managed to rebuild it with modern technology. He altered it to project a hologram and played a video of a "Christmas" festival, parade, and family gathering sharing gifts and dining.

They awed at the scenes and it appealed to them, but they had no idea what the celebration was nor what it was about. The videos were saved on the phone and Knox attempted to decipher their purpose or sentimental value but no information came with it. The only consequential word that recurred was "Christmas". It was about as far away from Light Day as it could possibly be, but the importance of both holidays was about equal.

They stared attentively, pondering over the sincere and silly imagery. What really caught their eye was the absence of fear. Where Light Day is a day of honor and earnestly grave worship, the mysterious Christmas seemed fun and lighthearted. They continuously saw a fat man dressed in red and white. The thought that perhaps he was a god whom the celebration was directed at fluttered in their minds. Even still, he didn't seem like a mean or frightful god who demanded respect, but one who liked all and gave them presents.

It made them sad, knowing that fun and peaceful things like that no longer thrived–let alone existed. Light Day was fast approaching; maybe the darkest time of year, and they'd have to put on their masks more than ever once it arrived.

Knox left not too long after that, but first stopped Peter to ask if he wished to join him in a sneaking mission to the Center of Sciences to steal a scanner planted around the perimeter. Knox knew that, if they went through with their far-fetched trip, the scanner would come in use to see if anyone was nearby within a mile's radius.

Knox was a well-known thief in the group, and very good at it, for that matter. Yet, he wasn't a rotten one, but a kind of New Age Robin Hood where he only stole from those with the highest means.

Peter agreed, not knowing what he was in for, but couldn't deny that the devise was indeed important.

When Peter returned home, he hear a ruffling noise come from the kitchen. It confused him, not necessarily alarmed him. The Guards would have surely been in the living room, and there was no sign that anyone broke in.

He went in there cautiously and found a German Shepherd exploring the bottom drawers, sniffing out food. Interestingly, unlike most other starving mongrels outside, he seemed fit and healthy. Most importantly, he seemed exceedingly friendly, did not make a sound, and went straight to Peter, almost so as to let him pet him.

Peter realized he must've come in through a hole in the kitchen wall. He petted him and considered keeping him. The dog smiled with his tongue out and decided he would. He chose to name him Dexter.

He stayed by Peter's side for some reason for the rest of the night. Perhaps the poor animal was just as lonely as him and needed a caretaker.

It was late, and, like usual, Peter went over to lay next to the fireplace. The dog did the same and they both dozed off to sleep.

CHAPTER 9

Darkness in "Light Day"

The unholiest celebration began: the twisted, backwards, serpentine annual event always to take place on each 22nd day of December. It was Light Day. As Peter awoke in the morning, he saw the streets empty and desolate. The festivities would not begin until darkness set in over the skies. Then would iniquitous knavery against all things good reign until the next day.

Light Day had replaced the once joyous, cherished Christmas; moved back three/four days to honor the solstice. Like Saturnalia of the past–which was ironically the origin of Christmas–Light Day hailed the longest day of the year, shortening. It was a day of the sun, the day of Anathea who manifested light in the universe and brought divine fire (wisdom) to mankind and returned. No longer would darkness and night continue to increase daily, but cut itself shorter and lesser over the all-powerful sun which she was. She "started the sun again"--reinvigorated her power over cold blackness.

Indeed, just like Saturnalia, it was a holiday of unrestrained revelry. The people still had to follow the laws, of course, but drugs, vanquishing of immorality and suspected terrorists/fear-mongers, reproduction of the fittest, mass displays of flags and propaganda, vandalism of those with lower credit, etc. were all highly encouraged. As peculiar as it sounds, the people believed that on that day, the literal spirit of Anathea descended unto and possessed every person of *good-standing*. To smite–perhaps even murder–the ungodly was she herself doing the deeds.

Many sacrifices were given at that time. It was mostly animals, but "ignoble" and "undeserving" people could also suffer the spilling of their blood. For a day called "Light", it was most certainly the opposite.

People would place decapitated heads of small critters: rabbits, birds, rats, mice, and the like beside their doors on porches. It was supposed to bring good luck and please the goddess

that they were sacrificing her "scum" secondary living beings; similar to pumpkins/jack o'
lanterns of the past.

Although nearly none knew of Christmas or Jesus, those caught mentioning either would
be harshly whipped into place; likely with twice as many lashes than usual. Their homes would
be swiftly raided, and they may've been tortured until they relented how they had knowledge of
the two words.

"Light Masses" would take place at night in Anathean temples. Peter had never gone, but
considered it at that point–not because he believed in them nor wanted to hear any of their
vicious, wrong preachings, but because they'd hand out copious amounts of drugs, Rapts, and
alcohol to each participant who attended it afterwards. They would hand out a year's worth of
ecstasy, more than Peter could ever need. The drugs simply had too much of a hold of him. Their
freezing, long hands had a tight grip around his throat and dependence, fake happiness seemed to
constantly suffocate him. It was an awful thing: to not only humor, but participate in their sick
congregations simply for a quick fix.

Peter knew Janet would be ashamed and look down upon him if she knew he was going.
He abhorred the drugs, but desperation to feel better in his situation and help him get through it
was too much to bear alone. He needed help, but could find none. Those small bags of Rapts
were his only source of numbness.

So it was, that Peter decided at 5:00 p.m. to go to the mass on the other side of the city.
He never much cared about the trains, instead preferring to walk alone and gather his thoughts.
They were therapeutic to him and relieved some of his gross stress. At that point, the streets were
roaring. People danced, while others beat the homeless and cursed them for their "irreligious"
ways. People took it upon themselves to break in and raid their neighbors' houses. Recall, that
private ownership was nonexistent. Every home belonged to the government, and to do such
things was fully permitted. People took to being their own guards on that day, and put their holy
laws into their own hands. Meanwhile, the World Guards wandered about, getting drunk and
laughing at the disgusting things done to the poor.

When Peter entered the temple, he was horrified, but not surprised. All the things he saw were commonplace, but the chilling air and settings he could never get used to. Inside was dark, almost like an Old-World movie theater. He could hear mass, fanatical screaming from outside and it nearly hurt his ears once in the main room. On the stage were an assortment of huge lit candles. Walking around them, with whips in their hands, were blindfolded nearly-naked women who chanted unintelligible hymns.

Meanwhile, the priest (of sorts) walked up with a rabbit in his hands. The rabbit was a symbols of Anathea's spirit. It was an innocent, harmless creature who people admired. At once, the priest sacrificed the poor animal, yelling "Here we honor your spirit and release it to your children!". He then sprinkled its blood into the crowd and the people tried to catch the drops on their faces. At that point, the crowd sounded almost like a frenetic riot. They screamed with happiness and then chanted "Hail Anathea! Hail Gabriel!" in sync.

The countenance of Peter was that of inexpressible sickness. The sight of it all almost gave him a panic attack and he felt intense nausea.

The priest then got the mad crowd to settle down, wherefore he read passages from the Will of Anathea. At the same time, "ordained" people in the front encouraged people to sing. These songs were understandable, but Peter rather not have known what the words meant, for they were evil indeed.

Peter closed his eyes for the remainder of the event, only hearing the deranged screams and preachings piercing his ears. At that point, he considered regretting going. The drugs may not have been an incentive to witness such madness at the cost of it.

Once he left, the ushers at the door handed him a sack of the prized drugs. Again, he leaned his face downwards as he grabbed it and left. Outside, he looked into it, not smiling like others around him. They were just another way of controlling him, used against him if he went against the Order.

That night, Zempher had invited him to come over; the reason being unknown. When Peter got there, Zempher led him to a bedroom where he showed Peter a small baby pine tree with a few candles hanging on it. Peter thought little of it, not understanding its purpose or meaning.

"Pretty spectacular, isn't it? I thought you'd enjoy it." Said Zempher.

"What is it?" Peter asked.

"It's a Christmas tree, like those of the Old World. People would decorate them with ornaments and lights in the Winter. They'd place presents under them on Christmas Eve and families would open them the next day."

Peter then thought it was very special. Something about it was precious and unsullied, yet he didn't know why. It didn't seem dark or dogmatic, but rather a symbol of goodness and charity.

"Is that what that is?" Peter asked, pointing to a small item wrapped in newspaper below the pine.

Zempher grabbed it and handed it to him, saying he'd enjoy it. Peter eagerly opened it and found it to be a medium-sized, blank, leatherbound journal. Zempher knew Peter had enjoyed reading the forbidden books and wanted him to write his thoughts in it–true, honest ones; not the sick and perverse publications he was used to composing.

Peter was elated and thanked him. He only wished he could give him something in return, but Zempher said his friendship was enough.

The two stayed together for a few hours afterwards. They sat about the tree while the old man taught him more about the legendary Christmas and how people once acted around it.

Peter's mind was like that of a child, for his brain became a sponge to absorb all the strange and new information that seemed important.

A few days later, Peter was back in his department. He was told to go down the hall to grab something when he passed by the newsroom with reporters and anchors. He had a brief idea for a moment. He thought about the possibility of breaking in somehow and broadcasting himself to the world, telling them what they needed to hear. They were always live, never recorded, and it didn't seem out of the realm of success. Surely, however, he'd be killed if he did such a thing. Slave camps were far too meager of a punishment for spreading false news in that manner. He quickly dismissed the thought but knew if there was a way to reach a large audience, that was the ticket.

He returned to the bunker later that night with Knox, Janet, Arra, and Zempher. They brought out an old map of the area while Arra examined it for the location of the island. She found the general area of where it could have been, then saw a port Northward where they could journey too and find a boat in good condition. It was about thirty to forty miles away and they knew it'd take them about two days to make the distance. There were no airships or hover trains that went to it, as it was a few miles away from the nearest small town that was abandoned. The risk was high, however. Snow was accumulating fast and there'd be at least a foot and a half within the next month. In the mountains, it grow at least twice that any longer, so they knew the sooner the better.

They thought together and debated amongst themselves. In truth, they'd have little to lose, other than government spying. Yet, being gone for days would mean skipping school and work which meant the government searching after them to investigate. If they were honest about their adventure, they'd immediately be sent to the camps. They'd have to think of some fallback excuse before making one step outside.

Janet stepped up to the table and began assigning duties and making plans. As pure and innocent as she was—even clumsy at times—she knew when to take action and was a determined young woman. She valued freedom as much as any of them and wanted to taste it for the first time, no matter the repercussions. Peter looked at her then in silence with a light smile on his face. He'd always admired her more than anyone. She was his only friend, but he'd have it no other way. She was all he needed and no other girl could be as good of a companion as her. A thought crossed his mind in that second. He considered whether he was falling in love with her; perhaps he always did. He thought about the hallucination he had with the two of them as a couple. Maybe it could have been his subconscious? He thought. That the scene arose from somewhere deep inside his mind he wasn't aware of. The feeling was warm and graceful, but he had to dispel it for the time being. There were more important matters to deal with, and liberation was the number one priority on all of their minds.

When the rest of the group left, and only Janet and Peter remained, she brought out a gift she had stashed in her backpack. She knew the mysterious Christmas had something to do with it, so she brought Peter something special. She provided him with an old history book she found earlier. She said she'd already read some of it and was amazed but didn't want to give any spoilers. He appreciated it more than any knew. He hugged her and they were face-to-face. Both may have thought about it at that moment (at least Peter), the two kissing. Peter ended up only thanking her dearly. Perhaps they both knew things would change too suddenly if they did. The risks they were considering taking, made it harder to consider a relationship. If they were separated at that point, the sting would be even greater than if they were still friends.

The reason the notion of presents didn't exist in the Order was because Gabriel was seen as the one, only, and greatest gift humanity could possibly have received. It was almost like an insult–gift-giving, that is–, for it devalued Anathea's gift of her son. It lessened the meaning of the dictator somehow. It makes no sense, obviously, but they were senseless people.

The two friends stayed in the bunker for the rest of the night. Once Janet fell asleep, Peter sat at the table and opened the book. He was awestruck with what he saw. It was as if he was reading the entire history of some other planet. He knew utterly nothing about what was written. He became fascinated by just how opposed it was to the narratives taught in school. Interestingly, as happy as he was that he was learning, he pondered with melancholy. He considered how wisdom appeared like a curse when one cannot spread it. What good was his newfound knowledge when he hadn't the ability to share it with the world. The people suffered; yet willingly, like sadomasochists, but they didn't need to if they only believed in the book. Peter was only partially free in his mind with the insight, but so long as others were strangers to truth, he'd always be trapped. Therefore, *correct* knowledge, spread across all borders, tongues, peoples, and times, makes right; but when only a few possess it, not only do they hurt, but live in the ignorants' hell.

CHAPTER 10

Monitoring The Enslaved

The following day, Knox awoke from his slumber in his substandard, silent home while Zempher remained asleep. Still in a daze from dreaming about his friends and the island, he noticed the time on the clock and realized he overslept.

Quickly, he threw on his Guard clothes of white armor and grabbed his rifle. He'd have to be swift, jump on the hyper-train, and make it to the camp before being late. There was no tolerance for being tardy.

He approached the tall steel gates about 15 minutes later. Other Guards were surrounding it, eager to scan his wrist, despite being well-acquainted with him. They didn't know if he'd committed a crime since the last day, nor could ever truly *know* him. There was no trust.

The residue of Light Day always remained for a few days–usually up to the 25th, oddly. The Guards were thus still in a celebratory mood and paid less attention to the slaves. Euphemisms and their gentle, yet constricting and controlled, language were all too familiar. To call his workplace a re-education camp was, although partly true, an insult for those trapped there. It was hellish; a most terrifying nightmare for those unfortunate enough to land themselves within the fences. The rebels, sometimes called "darkness-makers", were at the sole will of each Guard–the latter being free to punish them in any way they saw fit.

When sleeping, not working, or not *learning*, they stayed in crowded bunkers. There were usually 20 confined to a barrack about 40 by 40 feet in dimension. They only had seven beds each, so they were forced to share them, despite being only singles.

It was Winter, and like most others, the people within them were drastically freezing to death, as there were no heaters and they wore little more than mere thick rags. One could hear them at night while patrolling the grounds: their painful shrieks and desperate cries for help. It hurt Knox dearly, but the power to help was out of his hands–only the power to *whip*.

During the days, they frequently work in the fields, tilling the ground, harvesting frozen (sometimes rotten) Autumn fruits and vegetables, or repairing machinery. Since their shows were made of canvas and a small layer of leather, their feet froze. Many times, their toes would have irreparable frostbite damage. They'd be permanently black/dark blue, and they lost all feeling in them.

Those that couldn't walk or were too weak for the fields would be placed in some of the small factories there. They'd make alcohols or sort addictive pills. Everyone–men, women, children, elderly, and sick–had a place and a duty they were to fulfill.

They frequently starved to death and those who didn't were emaciated. Part of that was due to a real lack of food, but sometimes as a result of Guards stealing theirs for themselves. They often relied on eating wild rats or cockroaches who creeped into their filthy bunkers.

If one did exceedingly well with their education (the classes being mandatory in the early mornings and evenings), they had the privilege of printing and making Anathean posters to be distributed throughout the cities. They were sort of the "High-Siders" of the camps and could get more food, better clothes, and less cramped houses, depending on their skills and obedience. Nevertheless, if they–like anyone–worked slowly, talked back, or failed, they'd be whipped into shape.

The process of dealing with them was very systematic and there were solutions to everything. After whippings and beatings, if one still did not perform to expectations nor comply with orders, they would be brought into a room. In that room, nicknamed the "ego-death" treatment, they'd be strapped to a chair while a terrifying drug was injected into their bloodstreams. They'd further be forced to watch correct and horrifying videos. The drug affected their minds to feel absolute panic and shock. It was like having the worst possible trip on a tough hallucinogenic. No one dared to fight against the order, lest they be subjected to pure fear at its finest.

Interestingly, the slaves were never granted drugs or alcohol. They did not deserve to feel happy, as they were being punished under the authority of the goddess. Only the sinister drug of the ego-death treatment was administered under special circumstances.

Daily reading and prayers of the religion and its texts were mandated in a small Temple placed within the camp. If one chose to dedicate themselves to being part of the clergy, they could also rise in the ranks and perhaps even be released early. Seeing as they were usually rebels, however, this was obviously unheard of.

That day, there was a slave sitting against the wall of one of his shacks. Her body was frail with her bones sticking out. She wasn't exactly refusing to work, more so that she simply couldn't. She stared at Knox, having trouble breathing, not having the strength to muster the softest sound. Indeed, it was obvious she'd expire soon without intervention.

Another man, one of the Guards, shouted at Knox from a distance, yelling at him to keep order. Knox knew he couldn't go against his co-workers, else he'd get in more trouble than even the woman. The man got the attention of another Guard who looked attentively at the two. Knox was rightly aware that if they came over, they may have beaten the woman to death. With his heart weighing like a 100-pound stone, he knew he'd have to act for her to survive. He lifted up his whip and struck her twice–trying to do it as lightly as possible. He pleaded with her to get up and move for her own sake. Thankfully, she slowly got to her feet, nearly falling over and breaking an arm, and shuffled over to the factory. It killed Knox to do it, but he knew he had to.

At midnight, the Guards had a celebration of their own in view of the fact of Light Day. Because of their "venerable service", they could obtain some of the best alcohol in the Northwest and gourmet food. They were far more revered than the peasants.

As they sat in a hall, feasting, dining, drinking, laughing drunkenly, they mocked and made fun of the slaves. Knox simply sat there, not touching his food or drink. It was all unfair and wrong, he thought. The Guards were less than human, yet thought they were higher beings than any prisoner. They saw themselves as superior, supercilious men, beyond the comprehension of the lay peoples. They were inebriated with the alcohol of disdain.

While they were distracted and doing their own shenanigans, he slipped some wrapped cookies and cakes in his pocket; as much as he could. Later that night, while the majority of Guards were asleep, Knox patrolled the bunkers. He passed by one, filled with little children. They looked upon him quietly, hoping he wasn't coming to whip them for a cause they weren't aware of. Instead, he hastily handed them the small desserts, instructing them to tell no one. Their eyes lit up and, instead of hogging them for themselves and fighting, they were selfless and split it evenly amongst them. It was a beautiful venture to see with kids. They took care of each other and watched their backs when their lives were so gloomy. It was the only thing they could do.

As he made his way home the next day, he walked along the streets, seeing a crowd of people huddling around television screens through a building's windows. Curious, he went over to look. It was live footage of a riot that broke out on the other side of the country. They looked absolutely menacing, crazed, and blood-thirsty. The people around him cursed with countenances of fiery fury. As scary as they appeared, Knox understood they were doing the right thing and admired them. And yet, he found it strange just how cruel and unforgiving they were. He and his friends followed the same lines of thought, but none of them were violent. Even the guards seemed less viscous. Unknown to him, that riot too, was faked, planned, and staged.

About an hour later, Knox and Peter agreed to meet up behind a partially burnt no-long-in-use store to get the scanner. They brought their stealth packs, knowing it was impossible to get anywhere near the tower without them.

Peter was getting cold feet as they walked there and looked at the 80-story in the distance. It was a risky job–even with the stealth packs–and they'd never get their chance at escape if they were caught. Still, it was dire they obtained the tech so he toughed it out and was more than ready to run if needed to.

They finally approached the fence that surrounded the magnificent piece of architecture. Knox used a strong clipper to clip the steel fence wires. Lasers would have been ideal, but the light surely would've given away their position. It was pitch black out and the only light they were able to utilize were those coming off of the tower. Despite this, they both saw some small moving figure ahead of them, but couldn't quite make out what it was.

They both looked at each other nervously before saying, "Ready". They bolted, yet carefully and attentively, to the scanner with a red light flickering on it. They made it and Knox was about to cut it off from the post planted into the ground when, suddenly, they heard a whisper from seemingly a girl.

"Don't!" Said the voice.

They looked around and found her silhouette peering through the bushes.

Knox didn't take her seriously and finally cut it off. Immediately, a loud, piercing alarm went off and all lights turned red. They fled as fast as they could with the girl following them closely behind. Unfortunately, the spotlights shone down to them but the boys were safe with their packs. The mysterious girl, on the other hand, was not wearing one and her face was more than visible.

Sprinting as fast as they could, they eventually made it back to the store and hid in it behind moved isles. Knox found that the scanner no longer worked without power (which he expected), but knew he could fix it in a jiff. It was at that time that they finally saw the girl and conversed with her. She was furious at them for giving away her position, but happy to meet them nonetheless.

She explained that her name was Nym. She was eighteen, had mildly-long brown hair, and hazel eyes. Upon Peter asking why she was there, she said she was trying to escape. She had cancer and was originally in the hospital, but the Center of Sciences "stole" her to test experimental drugs on her cancer. Thankfully, and to her surprise, the drug did indeed work, so she was grateful in a funny way. Still, she needed to get out before they filled her or operated on her with god knows how many sinister drugs. She could have been made into a lab rat.

It just so happened that she was a rebel too.

"You're all stupid for even thinking about getting that thing." She said. "You could've gotten us all killed. What do you need it for anyway?"

"It's for personal reasons." Replied Peter.

She appeared to be a tough girl–hardened and able to handle many situations by herself. They decided to stay the night for good measure. Meanwhile, they talked about themselves and were intrigued at finding yet another person on top of Peter and Janet in such a short while.

She was obviously an experienced criminal; more so than even them. She had done innumerable illegal jobs in the past and didn't feel too scared about what had transpired a few hours prior, but not realizing her face was seen.

The boys considered telling her about their headquarters and letting her into their circle, but were still unsure about trusting her, despite proving she was exceedingly similar to them. She was stubborn, perhaps a little cold, and it was likely for that reason they were hesitant. However, as the hours passed on, she seemed to lighten up. It may have been due to her countless run-ins with other criminals that made her that way. They [criminals] all shared the same goals, but outlaws had always been outlaws–no matter the point in history. They likely betrayed her.

She had lost her house while at the Center; being given away to others, as per orders from the city government. Having no place to stay, Knox agreed to take her in. One can obviously see that he had a light, kind heart, having accepted both her and Zempher into his abode. Perhaps he was lonely as Peter, but more that he was just that generous.

Peter got up in the early morning before the others awoke. He had work in a few hours and wanted to get home before sunset.

Upon opening the front door, he found Dexter staring at him with a smile and holding a dead fox in his mouth. He walked up to Peter and dropped it at his feet. Peter thought it was quite the treat and petted him. The dog and he would surely grow very close.

Peter cooked it up and they shared it with one another on the floor, giving half of the meat and all of the giblets to the Shepherd.

CHAPTER 11

Winter's Toll

Early January had arrived; snow heavily coated the city, temperatures dropped into the single digits, and the time of suffering blossomed once more. It was a feared time of year for everyone in the slums and Low-Side of towns. Hardly anyone had heat and, save their blankets and wooden stoves (which only a few possessed), and the reaper came with a sharp, icy sickle.

To make it all worse, a famine had occurred during the year, leaving an even graver lack of food, and an abnormally cold, grating Winter plagued the territories. People found themselves blue in their homes, attempting to eat frozen rations from cans, and giving most of what they could to their children. They begged to go to work for some semblance of heat.

Widespread starvation was always common (even in the more temperate months), but that January would herald in the taking of more souls than the past year combined.

Despite all this, the people still rationalized that it was okay to die. They had a process in their mind that I like to call *sense-contortion*; meaning they could bend and reshape their rational falculaties to fit their beliefs, rather than the other way around. Instead of a belief influencing their thoughts, their direct thoughts on that belief could be contorted to further twist/distort both the belief and the thoughts together. For instance, the people originally–and always–believe Anathea to be the best, most merciful goddess of absolute, pure goodness. Yet, when hard times arise and they are literally suffering and slowly dying, the people, instead of realizing that their goddess and her attributes contradict each other, the people reconfigure their own beliefs on her to think that their punishment is noble and good, simply for the fact that it is happening to them. And yet still, when positive things do happen, they believe that it is because Anathea is wholly ethical–entirely forgetting all of the bad they've experienced. They are in a constant state of contorting their senses, trying to hold onto a belief that makes no sense–contradicting Gabriel's teaching that she demands objective, solid truth without doubt or individual interpretation.

Their senses were in a perpetual state of change, although they were not aware of it, because their egos and self-reliance were absent. Anathea and her actions took the place of their freethinking brains, so no matter what she declared or did, they accepted and justified it.

One may, by now, ask themselves why resources in a society working in overdrive were so scarce. The short answer is that neither trade nor businesses existed, and the supply chain was fully under the authority of the minuscule, yet most powerful, government. It was much like Mao's China in the 20th century.

The labor sector was predominately headed in the main city where the Aristocrats and the dictator dwelt. They were in charge of accounting for goods and redistributing them. In the vast majority of cities and towns throughout the world, there existed no departments to report their resources. It would simply require far too many buildings and government officials–the latter being very dangerous. So, the lead headquarters would, for example, tell Peter's city to process nails to ship throughout the country. It may work for a short time but, a shortage of metal in his city would mean that the town shrunk the nails and made them smaller in order to meet demands. Then, when the nails are sent away, they are unusable, and labor requiring them elsewhere ceases.

Now, take food and necessities. For the entire world, one (or a small group) must decide how much needs to be produced, how such can be done, and where they're needed most. Is producing wheat as important as building new homes? If so, where? Is providing medicines as important as constructing hospitals? If so, in what cities? No matter how large the central labor department is–and it was exceedingly small–no amount of people in a committee could possibly account for all the possibilities and factors that must go into planning labor demands and millions of distribution sites.

In order to measure needs and locations of such, there must be market prices and values of each good across the world. If one thing is more expensive in a number of places, and less so in others, it's clear who needs what. But, since all resources are owned by the government, there are no large-scale trades nor market prices. Without being able to gauge the monumental individual needs of everyone throughout the planet, the small government is clueless of how and where to distribute–let alone coordinate and communicate to each and every city/town.

Desperate, people in Peter's city (along with he himself), began to eat rodents, pests, and small creatures in order to substitute for the inedible, rotten and frozen food of months prior. He began to shed weight at a rapid pace and knew something had to change.

Peter sat on the bed in his room with a pen and his journal. He wrote his thoughts about the matter; the desperation of the people and endless, needless suffering. He wrote in the hopes that one day, a day long down in the future, if humanity did not fully destroy itself, they could see just how bad things used to be. Perhaps they'd learn from their mistakes; yet, if history has ever taught man one thing: it's that people continually don't listen to it. They remember history briefly, thinking they won't make past mistakes, only for them to either corrupt the past or forget about it entirely–perhaps out of ignorance or willing blindness.

To make it all worse, his father had fallen very ill from a dire strain of flu. He knew he needed medicine desperately, as the hospitals were too full, and he couldn't bear losing him, just as he did with his mother. He was the only family he had left and couldn't live with himself, if not for Janet and his new friends.

Acting fast, Peter reluctantly decided he'd have to steal from the High-Side of the Community Pantry. Indeed, his credit was well, but not nearly high enough to get the prized effective medicines. He didn't know what would happen if he got caught–which was a very likely scenario–, only that it'd not be good. He couldn't stand seeing and hearing his father moan and shout in agony while dying, though, and it was either a punishment on his part or the death of his parent.

While making the trip there, covering himself from the thick falling snow, he came upon a dead young man lying in the street. Assuming he died of the cold, he thought little of him, until he approached and saw him clutching a bag of a drug in his hand.

He didn't understand why, but it left a heavy impact on Peter. It both made him sad and scared about who he was becoming. Would he eventually end up like the man if he continued to self-medicate? It seemed like the only escape, but the escape of death brought about a complete opposite feeling of fright. It would make him evermore hesitant to take his Rapts, or at least increase the doses, from there on out.

As he entered the Pantry, he was given the band around his arm that indicated he could shop on part of the High-Side, but not acquire everything. Once about to leave, they scan what he picked and compare it to his credit. The only way past it was to sneak it. He tried to act inconspicuous. The cameras were surely pointed directly on him (as everyone else), with Guards at the entrance. He acted calmly and without care of surveillance, tricking them into thinking he wasn't up to no good. He walked past the medicines, quickly gazing at the one he needed. Looking forward, he swiftly nabbed it and stuck it against his belt and stomach. He then grabbed other items, to fool them into thinking there was a real purpose for him being there.

As he checked out, one of the Guards slowly walked over to him. Instantly, he began to sweat and considered sprinting out of the building as fast as he could if the Guard mentioned anything. He looked partly angry and demanded Peter pull up his shirt. He must've noticed the slight bulge. Peter then tried to run, but the man immediately gripped his arm tightly and dug it out of him. Peter squirmed but could not get free of the muscular Guard.

At once, he was dragged outside, where the Guard screamed for others to come over, exclaiming his crime. Passerby civilians, wanting to *do their part*, grabbed both of his arms and tore off his shirt and shoes. The Guard then stood a ways behind him and threw his whip as hard as he could, yelling obscene New Language insults at him. Peter cried in agony for each strike that was laid upon his person. He begged but was shown no mercy. The whip whipped at least five times, but Peter lost count while focusing only on the sharp pain. Finally, it stopped. He was commanded to never do such a thing again, else he be thrown in prison. He then scooped up his shirt and shoes, demanding he leave.

Peter, utterly freezing, numb, bleeding, and in anguish, ran home barefoot in the snow, upset about himself and scared for his father. To throw gas on the fire, his social credit score likely took a blow and he'd be monitored even more. He lay there, that night, tossing and turning in his bed, and having to lie on his stomach, until the following day when he'd have to resume work.

Once at the Department, he sat in his chair as blood seeped through his beck and ran down his suit. Surely, it was noticeable, but there would not have been one person in the building who'd bat an eye. Ironic, how the society formed off the basis of "altruism", seemed so selfish and egoistic not to help those hurt or in need. They correctly assumed what had happened to him and shrugged it off, knowing he deserved the treatment.

His boss then came over and told him to–this time very frankly–make up a story about criminals scheming to "retake" the Order. He was told to emphasize that such people and their conspiracies reinforced the need for a stronger military. His peers weren't even trying to mask their intentions anymore. Although, it could be said that it was a positive thing, just how much they were trusting Peter; perhaps they were willing to increasingly reveal more about corruption and illusion.

Notwithstanding that fact, Peter was furious and wanted nothing more to do with them. He knew, more sure than ever, that he was going to leave and never come back. He wasn't going to humor slave camps, prisons, nor death. He was going to the island, one way or another.

Meanwhile, Knox was in his house attempting to fix the scanner and power it back up. Nym came over to try to help him, being exceptional in gadgets herself. As she sat close to him while he tinkered away and focused on the metal, he looked at her and asked her her story.

She discussed the Order, how much she felt disdain towards it, but even relented that she was once an Anathea-ist when younger. This was extremely surprising to Knox, as she seemed well-grounded and to have her head tight on her shoulders. One would never expect her as having once been compliant in their ways.

She was apparently raised that way with her parents being young. She said, though, once her sister died about five years ago, she lost all hope in the religion. Her sister had awful credit, slacked in school, and never prayed.

"I'd be damned to think she went to any sort of "Hell"." She said. "That's what people tried to tell me. She was the most tenderhearted, kindest person one could meet. If there was some goddess above who saw her as not being good enough, then I say screw her and I'm more than willing to blaspheme her name. Besides, Gabriel has always left a bad taste in my mouth. At first, I couldn't put my finger on why I didn't like him. But now I see it clearly. He's an evil, self-centered bastard who only cares for himself and bathes in the suffering of his people; demanding praise for it! After her death, I never took Rapts again. It was strange, somehow my mind just clicked and a switch turned off: the switch from bad to good. I no longer wanted anything to do with Anathea and her government. It happened quickly and I've been a rebel ever since."

She had met other groups throughout the years, but they all seemed to leave her behind. They didn't show up to a usual meeting spot one time, maybe because they knew the location was compromised. She was encountered by a Guard–fortunately one in number–and got in a fight with him. She managed to knock him out but she'd never do it again. She almost died.

She knew big groups were more dangerous and susceptible to being caught, and it was likely for that reason none ever stayed with her.

They bonded quite well and the two seemed very fond of each other. Knox had more in common with her than any other person and she needed a companion desperately. The rebel's life was a lonely, despondent one.

Knox was continuing to speak with her when, out of the blue, she leaned in suddenly and kissed him. Obviously he was taken aback but secretly enjoyed it. She apologized but he said he didn't mind at all. She said she'd been solitary and isolated since her sister's death and he could sympathize.

He asked that she stay with him and that the two would be safe if she did so. She simply smiled and helped him fix the scanner for the rest of the day.

About a week later, Peter immediately leapt from his bed when the loud sound of sirens began to blare through his neighborhood. The lights in the district had turned red and something bad was coming upon the neighborhood. He (like all) knew well what it meant and feared it. Immediately following the alarm, a recorded voice came on, instructing people to get in their homes and stay there.

Peter knew what it was all about. It was a mass raid, likely due to the surfacing of rumors about illegal items/people hiding about. There was a sense of relief on his part, knowing that he hadn't–as far as he knew–did anything wrong, and they'd never discover the crawlspace beneath the house. He thought about going down there, but knew better. His absence would bring up suspicion and the camera in his television showed that he fled into a back room and disappeared. They'd come to find him in the home, either way.

He sat on his couch quietly as three Guards busted open the door. One held his rifle on Peter, telling him not to move, while the two others ransacked and destroyed the house, leaving it in ruins.

Peter took a huge sigh of relief when one said, "Nothing." and they ran back outside.

He then heard a couple people screaming. Curious, he looked out the window and saw a group of men being dragged out into the streets. A few other Guards behind them held piles of books and pictures in their arms. What happened next was interesting, and a new sight for Peter. They were tied behind their backs in a circle around a pole. They were then commanded to sit. One Guard, had a large poster in his hand, flipped it over, and wrote "Leave The Damned". He then taped it to the pole above them. The same man then brought out a baton, walked around the circle, and bashed each person's legs in–swiftly breaking them all so they could not again stand (let alone walk). They screamed in pain, praying that that alone was the punishment and they'd eventually be free, but that was sadly not the truth. Guards surrounded them and it was their duty to monitor the men until they finally, very slowly and painfully, died.

The Guards with the paraphernalia then dropped all of the items in front of them. The people stood outside of their doorways, watching attentively, and happy that justice had come. The Guard gripped his flamethrower, and burned all the items as the public cheered.

CHAPTER 12

The Sacred Dictionary

Peter had stayed daily by his father's side. He had been bedridden for the past week, lost a fair amount of weight, and made hardly any noises save incessant coughing. The bronchitis was acute at that time, distressing, and spreading. Dexter stood near, often licking his face in hopes of cheering him up. He must have sensed agony.

When Peter got home from work a few days later, he went to attend his father and check up on him. He found him asleep, but quickly noticed he wasn't breathing. In an instant, he jumped on him to perform CPR, but after countless compressions, he realized it was too late and he passed. Peter lay by his bedside and wept. He was his only remaining family and he'd have to be by himself in the house: alone, forlorn, and depressed.

He sat there for hours, staring at him and thinking of good memories, but regretting that he couldn't say goodbye. He knew he'd have to tell somebody, but he couldn't stand the thought of the Guards hauling the body over to the mass graves and burning his body. If only he got away with the medicine, he thought; or tried harder to raise his scores to purchase it. His heart sunk, and he'd have to rely on Janet even more.

With melancholy, he went to inform a Guard. Two of them, without saying much, came over and took him away. Death was far too frequent to get huffy over, and they were well-familiar with grim. They burnt the body, both because it prevented spreading of diseases, and because it was a morbid sacrifice to the goddess–*humans were formed from dust, thus shall they return to it*. Peter simply sat alone for the remainder of the night, trying to fall asleep and fantasizing about a new life. He missed his mother equally as his dad and wondered what it'd be like if they were both with him and he grew up with a typical family. Believing the same things as himself, they could have taught him innumerable extra things about the past and comfort him when he felt low. They were his rock and his friends would have to fill their place for the sake of his sanity.

A little later, Knox traveled with Nym to the bunker, feeling that she wouldn't give them away nor betray them. Surely, the rest in the group (save perhaps Peter) may not have agreed, but she was trustworthy and Knox, was a good judge of character, had high fidelity.

It just so happened that Janet and Peter were there, as well. Needless to say, she was as amazed at the place as much as Peter once he found it. She had attended other secret locations before, but nothing like theirs which contained so many striking items.

Peter had convinced Janet that she was safe and she paid little mind but Arra walked in shortly after and did not share their appreciation for a newcomer. She was confused and even a bit angered at Knox, thinking he was being foolish and they didn't need anymore people.

Knox, who admired Arra infinitely and had been longtime friends with her, spoke to her privately, explaining that it was okay and she desired to escape with them. She didn't like it but trusted her friend and didn't blame him for opening up his mind to a fellow "terrorist". Nym interrupted them, adding to Arra that she believed in the same cause and that, having already met the two boys, if she were to turn them in, she would have done it long before arriving. Arra finally accepted, praying that her explanation and word was true.

Arra showed her a map, but not the exact location of the island (even though she herself didn't fully know), but rather just the vicinity. Nym then intervened and told her that she was right but needed to alter the course to account for the strong Pacific currents. Arra was fairly impressed by her education and realized that she was right. If she had not said anything, they could have strayed far from the destination with it slipping under their noses.

Nym generously asked if she could bring anything else to the table, wherein Arra told her to bring as much supplies as she could muster and set her affairs straight to leave soon. Nym was happy to comply.

The entire group (Janet, Peter, Arra, Knox, and Zempher) met up the next day at Janet's home while her parents were away at work. Her family was a little more wealthy than Peter's because of credit, with a nicer house and better food, but, being in the slums, it was still a shanty home in a shanty town–as the old worlder's would say.

He contemplated telling Janet about his father but felt it wasn't the right time. He was grieving heavily and did indeed longed for her comfort, but they had more important business to attend to and he didn't want to waste their precious moments talking about it. He surely looked more despondent than usual and she may have seen it but didn't say anything. She was a keen observer of the world–more so than most her age–and she could read Peter better than anyone.

They had to act quickly and discussed the journey. Janet, although not knowing the fabled island as Arra did, was she who predominantly took action. She said how they'd have to slowly stock up on food and water, even if it meant temporarily starving. With hope, they could find fishing gear on a boat for food, hunt for a small time, and make it to their destination soon, lest they run out of water and die at their own foolish hands.

The rest were safe, except for Janet. She feared her parents finding out. They were extraordinarily adherents of the dogma and the possibility that they'd even turn in their own daughter to the Guards wasn't out of the question. Again, she realized just how ignorant and half-witted she was for them to be at her home. There were cameras planted throughout it in every electronic device and they made sure to discontent them all before getting into the nitty-gritty of their endeavors. They couldn't just block the cameras, as there were voice recorders hidden in them too.

Zempher had the idea of getting a weapon somehow–likely a gun. The group wasn't opposed to it, but it was impossible. Knox was the only one permitted to use a gun and there was no way to get it out of the camps. Even if they did, in some far away universe, the risk was simply too high; especially what they'd do with it. If they even pointed it in the direction of anyone, they'd be burned on the spot: camps were too small of a thing for people like that. The thought quickly faded away and banished from their minds.

That night, Peter went back to the crawlspace of his home for alone time: sitting down and listening to illegal music he borrowed from the bunker. It was like a drug to him, getting high but without any substance in his body, save the sweet frequencies that emanated from a little primitive device. As he lay there enjoying the sounds, he brought out an Old World dictionary that Zempher had given him from the Center of Proper Language Use. He thought it was strange that such a thing would be stored there, but perhaps they kept it as a reference to know what words were and were not allowed to speak anymore. Only a handful of eyes were allowed to look upon it there.

Many of the words were nearly unintelligible, but English had not changed as drastically so as to be entirely different. Most basic grammars still existed: proper pronouns, verbs, nouns, adjectives, adverbs… were still in use; it was mostly the meanings and definitions of words that had been altered. The more he read, the more he deciphered them and could speak as one from the 20th century. It was like the difference between 18th century and 20th century English. It was possible to speak and write in both ways, but one was harder to understand than the other. It was simply too new, too foreign.

Therewish Peter brought out his journal and attempted to form sentences of his own with words from the book. He wrote his opinions on the meaning of life.

Like many past philosophers, he believed all people desired happiness–whatever that meant; but every person had their own interpretation of it and common thought changed with each era. In the mid 20th century, the ideal life was working hard; having, raising and providing for one's family; contributing to one's society; and following/believing in universal or cultural values. Before that, religion dominated the sphere of influence over the people, where they shared the same beliefs, but it differed from Anathea-ism. There was order then, but the punishment of stepping out of line for one sole person's definition of order didn't result in burning to death, nor did ineffable suffering come out of the hands of any major religion.

Most importantly, however, individualism, liberty, and freedom in the previous, sovereign United States was what was so alluring. There was something about it that made it appealing: the fact that one was not forced to do anything major, punishment was not so severe and arose from justified means or crimes with a fair, impartial trial. People were encouraged to think on their own and believed as they wished. Yet, it was not as Gabriel and his disciples said–there was no anarchy. The country was the greatest and most powerful that ever existed and the will of each person mattered; but, people walked in different lines. They had the ability to do as they pleased so long as it didn't infringe on the prosperity of others. They could choose their own jobs, speak whatever they wished, disagree, protest when they felt injustice. Above all, they lived without perpetual fear.

The people in Peter's world had eyes; they were open and healthily working, yet blind at the same time–a strange, but adequately said, oxymoron.

As he sat there in tranquility, he pondered about the trip. He doubted himself about it and whether or not he should go with them; not at all because he didn't want to nor not be free, but because he felt deep down that he had a purpose–one to help the people in some form. He was at a complete loss whether he could even do that and whether or not it was a good idea, but it was indeed a most admirable thought. He leaned towards staying, as arduous as it was, but kept it to himself and wouldn't tell the others. He still happened to write his considerations down in his journal, with the hopes that maybe someday people would understand his difficulties. It'd take more than the strength he possessed to abandon his loved ones and forsake the one chance of liberation.

Suddenly, he heard a knock on the door from above. In an instant, he switched off the music and lights, and the room became deaf. He waited for a few minutes, but heard nothing. This eased him as, if it was a Guard, they'd break down the door soon after if not answered. Reluctantly and slowly, he ascended and opened it. To his surprise, it was Janet. An ocean of relief overcame him and he couldn't have wished to see anyone but her. She seemed distressed and needed to talk to him.

Apparently, her dad had found an old DVD player hidden away in her room. She stuttered when he did and, after threatening to turn her in, she swore to him she didn't realize it was illegal and played dumb. The prophecy of her deranged, dangerous parents came true. They said little and seemed to believe her–or give acknowledgement of her plea at the very least. Thankfully, they hadn't done anything for a couple of hours and she had a reprieve, but told Peter they needed to leave soon nonetheless.

Peter swore, both to himself and her, that he'd never let anything happen to her; and if it meant hiding her perpetually himself in the crawlspace or bunker, he was more than willing. Or, they could simply run away, just the two of them, at any time, and desert the god-forsaken dystopia. He couldn't bear the thought of her being enslaved, imprisoned, or killed. He die for her, and wouldn't relent where she was, even if he was tortured.

Janet hugged Peter, caring deeply for him and his kindness. She then put her arms around his shoulders and leaned in for a kiss. Peter was dumbfounded. It was his first kiss and he'd not have it be any other way with some other girl. He knew then that she felt the same love towards him and stirred his emotions from grim to warmth. She simply said, "We'll take care of each other.".

CHAPTER 13

Hiding Hannhia

It was midnight when Zempher left his home. He felt lonely and needed reassurance from the *correct* things in the bunker that reminded him of the *good ol' days,* as he'd put it. Of course, it was past curfew so he'd have to be attentive. Large intercoms would announce the set time of staying home at midnight, with the sounds blaring through the entire city. They'd often make other pronouncements–such as instructing people to contribute, have faith, act upright, be attentive to your neighbors, etc.

Unfortunately, half way through the city, it dawned on him that he forgot his stealth pack–a grave mistake.

Instead of going back and risking walking down the streets again, he decided to stroll quickly through the dark alleys for good measure. Even still, he knew there were cameras watching in some places so had to ensure that he didn't bring attention to himself and tried to walk behind objects. Unknown to him, he was entirely exposed and was constantly being monitored. The decision to not go back would be one he eventually regretted.

He passed many homeless, *cancerous* people in between the midnight buildings. It made him sorrowful and it reminded him of the pain he once felt while without a home and on the streets. None of them deserved their situation and he yearned to help them; it being improbable.

On the side of the highrise structures, about a hundred feet in the air, he saw the 20-by-20 feet glowing screens of Gabriel and his followers handing out food to the poor and reading them scriptures. They played endlessly–all day and night. Other screens portrayed giant single eyes with a text below it reading, "Anathea sees all. Do not disappoint". Some had hands on the sides of the eyes. One would have a word on it saying, "Law"; the other saying, "Obedience". It was a sight to behold: perpetual paranoia of people watching, as a schizophrenic would believe. Yet, it was all real and no delusion. People were always being recorded and and sense of privacy was a thing long past.

It was then that he heard loud footsteps from a distance. He thought he may have been a derelict, but at once noticed it was a Guard. He must have been tipped off that he was walking down there. Zempher quickly hid behind some garbage cans. He then heard a yelp.

Peeking from behind, Zempher saw a homeless man being beaten against the wall. The Guard must have mistaken the poor man for him.

"No wandering after curfew!" The Guard shouted as he hit him in the stomach with the butt of his rifle. The Guard ought to have known he was required to live on the streets; that he wasn't an ordinary fellow, but they had no conscience. Notwithstanding that, they were still not permitted to roam around, so it may have been for that reason that he was confused.

Finally, as the yelping ceased and the Guard left, Zempher approached him to help. The man lay there with blood gently seeping out of his mouth and had trouble breathing. Zempher put his torso and head in his hands, telling him he'd be okay. The man's visage was one of confusion. Why would someone help a cancer? He asked Zempher, who said that he used to be one of them and knew their worth. The man said nothing. His lungs gradually, yet in a moment, stopped lifting and his eyes closed. He was dead.

Zempher lamented his death. The man was but only a lamb who'd done no ill-will against anyone. He deserved life, where Zempher was the one who was at fault. The two had their fair share of beatings on the streets and it was likely only one of many occasions that the man suffered. At least he was finally at peace; in a Heaven removed from the bastard "Anathea".

The Guards were some of the most respected people in society–sometimes even more than those with outstanding credit. They preserved all facets of ideology and doctrine; keeping those in check and ensuring that people stayed in line. It was all the more surprising that such "upright" people were those who abused their power the most. They could beat down anyone before their faces, without a sliver of objection.

Luckily, Zempher was close to the end of the alley, easily able to enter the outskirts without being caught again. He laid the man down and covered him with his torn, dirty blanket.

Meanwhile, Peter was also wandering along the back streets when he noticed the secret symbol of the white hand with a candle on a cellar door with rotting boxes around it. Funnily, it was open and not as hidden as it should have been.

He made sure to look both ways down the alley, making sure no one was nearby. He walked up to it and peered down, wanting to walk down the wooden stairs. It was completely silent and seemed to have no one in it. Finally, he decided to hurriedly go down just to see what it was about.

The second he entered, he found why there was no noise. It looked like a makeshift cabaret inside but it was completely burned down; every inch of it. Frightening burnt bodies littered the floors with the deceased appearing to have run away from the flamethrower's wrath. It was no longer a mystery why the place wasn't hidden the best. The doors were likely kept there and not sealed up to make an example out of the place. If others stumbled upon it, they'd see their fate of partaking in such activities.

He was then in his home sleeping when he was awoken by the sound of a crying baby. He couldn't make out where the sound was coming from, and paid it no mind, until a woman began screaming at the top of her lungs.

Peter leapt to the window and saw a Guard walking towards the house. Before he could enter, he saw a flash in the other home and a loud gunshot. Another Guard walked out of the door to meet the other one and they oddly went back to patrolling the town. At the same time, the baby continued crying incessantly.

Peter waited a good minute and could bear the thought of what happened and the state of the baby. Once the coast was clear, he snuck over to the home. As he slowly pushed the door open, he saw blood splattered over the living room walls. There was a woman, shot dead on the floor with her pants down, looking as though she'd just given birth. Behind her a little way, was a small, tender newborn lying on a soft blanket.

After picking it up, he immediately knew why the wicked murder happened. The babe didn't have a barcode on her wrist and the mother gave birth to her naturally and not in the Department of Breeding; nor without their consent. It was the first illegal human he'd ever seen. One born with the original sin of being born in the first place.

Babies–even legal ones–were considered the lowest of "acceptable humans"–even lower than very old people. Their ignorance, lack of experience, wisdom, and piety, left them no more than mere half-humans, half-beasts. It was only after they were at least partially grown that they gained recognition. It is therefore least surprising that they left her to die.

Peter, being the caring and empathetic boy he was, immediately wrapped her up to keep warm and took her quickly to his home. He placed her in a back room and attempted to sound-proof it as much as he could, so as not to draw attention. He put boards against the windows, made a makeshift cradle for her with high walls lined with thick blankets.

He tended to her the whole of the following day; feeding her mashed up canned fruits, coddling her, and trying to make her laugh. Still, despite these things, she continued to cry as any baby would do. He knew something had to be done. She would surely attract suspicion and he couldn't keep her indefinitely–especially because of work.

He chose to take her speedily to the shack at night, knowing it'd be a much safer and secure place. At the foot of the mountain, he looked back to see a Guard coming towards him, likely hearing the cries. To his relief, the Guard had not caught sight of them, but was indeed following them. He began to sprint, trying to lose him as best he could. Thankfully, he made it and immediately entered the tunnel, covered it, and sealed the bunker. It was much more sound-proof than his humble home.

Providentially, Arra, Janet, and Knox were there. They were confused, obviously, but once Peter shouted that he was followed, they all shut their mouths right away.

Knox had established his own cameras above, and they could see all the happenings. Sure enough, about fifteen minutes later, as they focused on the TV, they saw the Guard bust down the door above. He wrecked the place, scourging it for any trace of Peter. They feared for their lives but knew it was unlikely they'd find the tunnel or get through the reinforced metal door.

After a good while, the Guard left. Yet, the camera suddenly went out and they heard banging coming from the floors above, like something was crashing.

They remained there until morning, hoping that by then they'd be safe. While doing so, they talked about the situation of Peter's newfound friend. They were at a complete loss on how to deal and take care of her. Zempher was the only man with time on his hands and he'd have to stay there with her–at least until they figured out a plan. Janet brought up the fact that she needed a name. They all gave suggestions but decided that Peter should have the final say and chose. He eventually came up with "Hannhia"--his mother's name.

While waiting, Nym told them about the past rebels she once knew. She said how they were similar to her newfound one, but much less caring. They were all older gentlemen at least twice her age and they, for the most part, looked after only themselves and paid little regard to each other. For that reason, she greatly admired her new one for taking her in. Arra, Knox, Zempher, Peter, and Janet were closer to each other than even their own parents. They had a bond with each other under a common goal and mindset. They weren't like other rebels of their kind and oddly younger. This made her surprised, since the youngest people were always those led most astray.

The group's thoughts towards her were finally reciprocated. It brought joy to them that Nym existed and there were others out there like them; though concealed and tucked away in remote, unknown areas.

While they slept, she lay with Knox and they looked into each other's eyes. They may have well been officially dating and in truth, love is what they all needed most.

She asked if he'd abandon her eventually like the others had. It was irrational, and she knew it, but she'd been hurt so many times that she needed the reassurance.

Knox simply put his arms around her, saying he'd never met someone like her. They were like two peas in a pod in terms of thoughts, but not exactly in personality (which wasn't a bad thing). He promised her and said they'd leave the hellhole and she had to have hope in that. Their position in Gabriel's underworld would soon pass.

Once they emerged above ground, they found the shack completely burned, almost to the ground. There were still charred walls standing, but far too low to hide anything, save the couch which was the only important thing. They knew they'd have to use their wits more and be ever careful. In a way, they were actually happy that the Guard set it ablaze. The shack would draw far less suspicion from then on, and no one would think anything of it.

CHAPTER 14

Misguided Company

It was about mid-Winter and school had finally ended for the year. Interestingly, unlike in the Old World, school only lasted for a few months: from September 'till January. It was this way in order that the students could work and assist the government for the remainder of the year. It made no difference for Peter, however, as he was already working full-time and had a free pass from attending school. He didn't know what was worse–being indoctrinated on a daily basis or being the one who indoctrinated citizens himself while tiresley going against his morals.

Most kids loathed going into the workforce and enjoyed school–both because people (especially youths) naturally don't prefer labor and because they begged for more knowledge of how to properly live life and become good citizens. The adults, meanwhile, felt somewhat the same inside, yet outwardly represented themselves as savoring work since it was an "altruistic" thing and aided the Order.

They celebrated the final day with a school party, sort of in the likeness as Light Day, but not so hallowed nor important.

The bash was the only day of the school year when the students didn't directly learn anything; but that didn't stop the indoctrination. Everyone in the building went to the gym. After a long oration by the principal, the festivities began. It started with a game. The students would form a circle and go around saying quotes from the dictator's book. The person who could recite the longest one won.

There were less horrible scenes. They all drank, danced, and ate good food that the government supplied. Artificially sweetened candy was also passed around made predominantly from bugs. Other activities included dodge ball, where each person who got out was required to name a sin they had committed over the course of the school year–so long as they weren't major, the rest of the children forgave them.

The end game was the straw that broke the camel's in terms of fun for a normal person. A hare was then brought out and released; it was tradition. Whosoever caught the hare won. The crowd would then return to the bleachers while the winner stayed down and a table was brought before him with a knife laid on it. The student was then to sacrifice the poor creature. Upon doing so, the crowd stood up and cheered. That marked the end of the year and they swiftly left afterwards.

That day, Peter sat in his home alone, again, saddened and discouraged as usual. To his surprise, Janet came over to pay a visit when he finally confided that his father had died. She felt doleful and comforted him the best she could. In a sense, she could relate. It was a terrible thing to say, but her parents may as well have been dead. She had not one thing in common with them and was sure that they didn't love her the way they should have. To cheer him up, she asked that he'd come over to her house the next night and have dinner with her and her family. He agreed, liking the gesture and wanting to act thankful, but inside, he wasn't fond of it. He liked her parents no more than she herself and didn't want to bite his tongue while around them. He'd have to put on a mask in front of them, lie, and hide his inner detestation of every word that flowed out of their mouths.

As promised, Peter came over the following day. Janet was excited upon opening the door, of course, but the parents did not. They seemed almost disappointed in Janet for doing such a thing and looked at Peter as though he was cross-eyed. They were nice to him and treated him as a welcomed guest, but it was obviously just a show. They, like everyone else, were awful liars.

They offered him to sit at the table, as they did, when Janet's mother brought the food. Most of it was canned slop, but having good credit, the main course was a wild goose–which Peter was more than happy to dig into. It was the best food he'd had in months and began to not regret the situation as much.

All went well at first, until they pressed Peter on his job. They'd ask if he was happy with it; wherewith he joyfully agreed that it was a noble and fulfilling job. They'd then inquire about all of his duties. Knowing they should have heard the truth, but that it'd instantly backfire and get him in trouble, he lied and said they were reporting the truth of Anathea-ism and honoring the authorities. They seemed pleased with the response.

Janet's father was a surveillance technician. He installed cameras and other devices wherever they were needed in the city. He knew more than anyone about the scope of privacy and its unsuitableness. He explained (more like exclaimed with delight) that they were working evermore tirelessly to find wrongdoers. He said how Gabriel wanted it that way. Gabriel had a right to oversee all happenings in his world; that way, he could find and repair faults wherever they popped up in order to continuously make the Order immaculate.

He asked Peter if he had enough cameras in his house, as though it was a completely normal question. He commented that there can never be enough and tried to play it off, saying he'd need it if someone ever came over and tried to do *inappropriate* things–not necessarily Peter. He told the father he had about six and it made him impressed.

"Good man," He said. "We have about the same number here. In the same way that Anathea sees all, so should the government on her behalf. They help do her services. What is a society without order? Monitoring, observing, and dealing justice. That's the only solution."

Peter just stared at him without expression. He knew that was dangerous, disastrous thought and killed all notions of individual happiness and freedom. Having no choice, he nodded.

He left shortly afterwards after enduring ridiculous monologues by Janet's crazed parents. They did seem to change their perspective on Peter, however, and were shown to lighten up on him when told about his job, "beliefs", and obligations. They appreciated his devotion to the Order and responsibility of keeping it solidified.

On his way home, he saw a new technology that must have been set up. It was a large platform attached to an obelisk with a powerful beam on top shining into the night sky. The platform produced a massive hologram that made it seem like a giant stood on the ground. It was a type of businessman walking back and forth. He talked out loud to an absent audience, yet looking down at Peter, explaining why it's important to take Rapts–as they were "healthy and brought good will", respect their leaders, be altruistic and attend their jobs, and listen to people like him–for he knew the *right/correct way to live*. He continued, saying, "In the darkest situations, Gabriel and Anathea bring light and hope; trust in them. The more you suffer, the richer you will be in glorious Heaven". He concluded with, "Remember, an exalted world relies on you. Do your part. Right makes might."

It was one in the morning when he got close to home, but decided to take a detour. There was an abandoned Old World railway outside the city and presented an excellent view. He'd gone up there a few times in order to clear his mind and let himself contemplate. It felt like a minor escape, seeing the city from a distance, realizing he was no longer a part of it; if only temporary.

It was a tough climb through the thickets and metalwork, but he finally got to the top and rested there under the moonlight. He looked onwards below, seeing the huge buildings with smoke and gentle fires coming off of them. Then there were the obelisks that shot beams into the air and indicated there was indeed a magnificent city in his location–yet one that would be only fair-sized a century ago. He saw the ariships above, hovering over the city with their spotlights moving in all directions, examining the ground and scouting out unpermitted activities.

He sat, he fantasized about the world back when. What it must have looked like, smelled like, sounded like. Did they have structures as great, yet gloomy as his? He wondered what it'd be like to not be paranoid, to not fear anything, and believe what he wished. What was leadership then? And who ran things? He had never known anyone save the dictator. He pondered how freedom could possibly exist, for he'd never seen it: only what they called "Order". Could order and freedom coincide? How? He was told freedom was synonymous with anarchy. He pondered if there was somehow truth in his past hallucination and that his books opened some type of third-eye so he could even conjure up these thoughts and questions.

He lay back and stared at the stars above the smog and continued to imagine a place far from the noose and whip–a place where he could live his life with Janet; just the two of them, away from ego death and iron rule.

A few days later, the friends met in the bunker, listened to music, and talked about all the absurd things they had seen in the past days. Knox and Zempher then walked in. One seemed jubilant; the other, nervous.

Knox told everyone that he had something to show them. He zipped open his suit and presented a small gun before them. They were all shocked and scared at the same time, commanding that he said where he obtained and why. He said how he managed to sneak it out of one of the camps. It was hard, but far easier than a rifle or flamethrower. He thought they'd need it just in case once they made their trek to the coast. At the very least, they could use it to hunt. The entire group looked at him angrily. It was indeed a valuable asset, but if they got caught with it they'd all be killed on the spot. Then Zempher stepped up.

He told them how he'd been drafted into the military. It was the only position that the homeless were allowed to acquire. He was terrified of it and so was the group. They all knew, with his age and health, he'd never make it in there. His body would fail him after a week in bootcamp. Physicality aside, he wanted nothing to do with the people that had perpetually beat him his whole life.

They unanimously agreed that they'd have to leave soon and before that happened. They couldn't lose their friend–especially a precious rebel like themselves. The journey would be perhaps equally hard on Zempher. Twenty miles through freezing weather and snow was easily durable to the group, but not so with him. They could only hope of his success and that he wouldn't slow them down.

Peter went up to Arra a few minutes later. He handed her a 2020s style camera and asked that she record what went on in the Division of Food Security. She was confused and extremely reluctant. God knows what would happen if she got caught and interrogated about it. She asked him why, but he didn't say much nor gave a real answer, other than saying she needed to trust him. She did trust Peter, and took his word for it that it was something important. She grabbed it and put it in her suit.

About the same time, Nym was walking to Knox's house. It was still before curfew so she of course saw no threat. Unbeknownst to her, not wearing a stealth pack at that moment would prove detrimental.

She was still oblivious to the fact that her face had been spotted when at the Center of Sciences and she was in inconceivable danger.

She approached the house–no more than three-hundred feet in distance–when, out of nowhere in the darkness, an airship swiftly flew over her. They beamed their spotlights straight at her and shouted, "Halt!".

Her immediate reaction was to run but she knew that, if she tried, she'd be shot in an instant. Fear struck her ears and her heart sank lower than it ever had.

Meanwhile, Knox was waiting on his deck for her when he noticed the incident. Like her, his heart felt exceedingly heavy, but he wasn't aware of what was happening–only that it was bad. In an instant, he ran to her as fast as he could.

Then, he got tunnel vision and time slowed. Right before he made it, she was shot in the back.

He yelled out and quickly grabbed her in his arms before she fell.

The ship then demanded that he get away from her immediately, else he would too be killed.

They both looked each other in the eyes while tears ran down their faces. She softly, out of breath, told him sorry and that she loved him. Before he could mutter any response, her eyes closed and she took her final breath.

Again, the ship gave another warning and he had to force himself to let her go.

He desired his rifle at that moment, to shoot the Guard above and seek revenge. His first love was already absent and he felt immense heartbreak. He got the strength to semi-quickly walk away, all the while looking back at her. Another Guard on the street then came and lifted her over her shoulder. Fury boiled in his cauldron of a stomach and he was ready to run and punch the Guard, which was odd for him, seeing as he wasn't a violent person. Nevertheless, he had to restrain himself. There was no use in him dying as well.

He mourned her death the rest of the night, nearing overdosing on Rapts. That was the final straw he thought–they were leaving soon and never looking back.

CHAPTER 15
Flight

Over the course of four days, the group slowly began to bring more food, baby food, and essential resources to the bunker. They were already making it by with the little food they had as it was, but knew they'd need to bring as much as they could muster. The trip would be exceedingly short, but how long they'd have to stay on the boat–and even on the island–without necessities was out of their knowledge.

They had two military-grade backpacks, but Knox fashioned three more out of miscellaneous supplies he'd gathered over the years. So killed a kid he was, he may as well have been a master machinist. He could take a block of steel and, with the right tools, could make a good gun out of it. He was already more than privy in restoring Old World tech, even though he had to make the parts himself. He was truly a savant for his age.

While doing so, Peter slyly took the so-called Iphone tucked in there and hid it in his pocket. He knew it'd come to his advantage soon, but could not slip his plan to any of them. As well as that, he grabbed a handful of smoke balls. They were used by the World Guards only and Knox must have also snuck them out of the camp. Once thrown, they released an invisible gas that left the victims unconscious for a few hours. Completely non-lethal, but powerful. Knox must have held onto them in case Guards stumbled into the tunnel and they needed a swift escape. Only Peter knew what they'd be for.

Importantly–perhaps equal to rations, they brought droves of Rapts. They'd have to ween off of them, but, if they suddenly stopped cold turkey, they'd have no strength or morale to do anything. The withdrawals would be excruciating. They may as well been bedridden for days without them.

They planned to leave two later and had to make proper arrangements for their duties. Peter, Arra, and Knox informed their bosses that they were ill. It was not a likable decision and their credit scores would have slightly gone down; but regardless, credit would mean nothing once they entered the woodlands. Thankfully, Janet was out of school and Zempher had yet to enter the military so they needed not have excuses.

Peter, hurting himself, had to say goodbye to Dexter. The dog looked at him happy as usual but turned his head in confusion while the boy spoke to him. He desperately wanted to take him, but knew he wouldn't stay quiet and his barks would surely give away their positions. Even though he needed more, Peter left him some of his canned meat and bugs to keep him healthy. On his knees and petting him, he said one last farewell.

They were all equally concerned about Hannhia. The temperature was still in the single digits and they'd have to protect her as much as they could. Luckily, they had a heated blanket powered by a long lasting battery and would allocate it to her, for she needed it the most. They also brought powdered milk for her and New World "formula", despite how bad the latter was. Janet could also try to feed the newborn herself.

The day finally came when they met up one final time, prepared to be on their way. They all asked where Nym was and Knox just looked down quietly with a sad disposition saying she didn't make it. The group knew what it meant. They all felt sorrow and grief, but knew what they were in for–even Nym herself. They played the most dangerous game and she just wasn't as lucky. It was most sorrowful seeing how close they were to potential liberation. They all knew she was in a better place.

They threw on their packs and readied their gear. They stared at each other nervously, yet also faintly excited. The trip would be more than risky. Janet was the only one of the bunch who had nothing to lose–given she returned soon, but the rest of them could face consequences. That was not even considering the fact that they made it without being caught, found a boat, and actually located and landed on the island safely. They all thought about their families; the only things they'd miss from society. Even Janet did, despite not liking her parents. A child, deep down, always cares about their family, even when no attention is given to them. Still, they had to do it. Their families would never understand them. They were all swallowed up in the beast that was Anathea-sim and yet enjoyed it. The group would not be swallowed. They would not grow old and die in a world of madness, fear, and death. Either way, whether they succeeded in their mission or not, they would eventually die; it was worth doing so at the possibility of salvation.

They walked together further up the hill until they reached the summit. It was time.

After a short ways, they finally passed the smog that lingered in the air. For the first time, they could breathe easily. The air was fresher than they had ever tasted and they stopped to admire and take it in. Snowy clouds hung over them, but the sky seemed much lighter; much clearer and brighter; glowing even, despite being dark.

The deeper they got, the more unique and beautiful everything became. They'd never seen so many living and flourishing plants and birds before. It was truly a beautiful sight–one most appreciated by people such as themselves.

They all were in shock when they came upon bushes of wild blackberries. They were not fresh, nor rotten. Frozen from last Summer, they hurried over to them, threw them in their mouths, and sucked until chewable. They savored them as a thirsty man in the desert begs for the magnificent taste of dirty water. They spent hours there; finding as many as they could and stuffing their bellies. They were wasting time and finally had to force themselves to go on.

The sceneries and refreshingness continued until the brink of nightfall when they were forced to camp. Hannhia and Zempher were doing surprisingly well for their exposed and fragile bodies. The group was making good time–about twenty miles completed–and figured they'd arrive in another day and a half or so.

Around 5:00, they decided to set up camp. Fashioning snow caves would have been ideal, but they neither had the time nor strength to. Thankfully, they had brought two blowup tents that could keep them warm, no matter the temperature. They also had thin weather-sheets, similar to Old World compact and lightweight emergency blankets, but far more effective.

It was finally dark about that time and they'd already set up a good-sized fire. As they sat around it and discussed all the things they'd do once they made it, Peter looked back and forth between Janet and the flames. He pondered and lamented over Janet; staying with her, growing old as a liberated couple, raising Hannhia together, and perhaps having a child of their own. It made him sad and happy at the same time: sad about losing her, and happy about the thought of her long-awaited independence and safety. He couldn't brace the thought of losing her.

As the skies got darker, Zempher told stories of the Old World and some of the things he remembered. He said little of it before–both because his memory was slowly failing him, and because it hurt him too much to consider all the grand things that used to be. He was only in his early twenties when Gabriel was introduced to the world and he recalled only glimpses of life before.

He told how the world was never perfect; indeed, the early 21st century was no utopia, but it may as well have been one compared to their time. People were not happy in his youth. So many things seemed backwards, no one trusted their governments, people were at the epitome of division, and hatred abounded. And yet, despite all of that, people took their lives and situation for granted. They didn't realize just how much worse things could become and, ironically, it was due to themselves giving such a dark man as Gabriel power. They all had the ability and knowledge to solve all problems, but they could simply not see past their egos and self-centeredness. It was strange. People then, every one of them, thought they were leading the correct way of life and all other people with different opinions were wrong. As well, they continued to buy into leaders who promised solutions, yet distrusted all opposing prominent figures. In a sense, their mentalities weren't so different as Anathea-ists; however, their desperation grew so large that a person or newly created ideology guaranteeing a blemishless society could easily overcome all of their hearts. Gabriel promised unity–what they desired most–and somehow brought it to them in their schismatic, hysterical state. They were utterly vulnerable to their inner beastly thoughts arising from their hatred.

Janet and Peter were the last to stay up and talk. She handed him a letter she got from the school about a few days before. It was to inform her of her new job at the Center of Sciences. It was a real job and she'd be forced to participate. She laughs at the thought she'd ever go. She'd rather escape on her own, or even die, before working with such iniquitous, immoral people.

Peter greatly admired that and wished he would have done the same. He venerated her will to oppose the baleful government, even if she didn't have a choice. Still, he was doing the same thing–escaping, and she liked him just as much for that reason.

Once Janet went to bed, Peter decided to stay up later, alone by the warm, crackling air. He brought out his journal and tore a page off of it. He wanted to write a letter to Janet, telling her how much he cared and prayed for her. For being a tough, yet sensitive boy, he freely and earnestly spewed out his feelings. It was cathartic, explaining every emotion he had–most of which he never had the opportunity to tell anyone.

He put it in-between the first page and cover of his journal, which he then slipped deeply into her backpack, hoping she'd find it at the proper moment.

The following day started off as good as the previous. They woke up early, took some Rapts, drank coffee, and hiked quickly. Unfortunately, Zempher began to straggle and their pace slowed. His body was weakening, not being used to such physical hardship, and his hands were succumbing to severe frostbite. He'd force them to stop about every third of a mile and they knew that keeping such speed would take them additional full days before getting to their destination. They ultimately made the decision to create a sled and drag him along on it. It would still slow them down, but it was better than him walking by himself.

As they crossed a frozen river and came out on the other side, they saw an animal staring at them in close range. They had no idea what it was, never having seen such a beast. Unbeknownst to them, it was a wild stallion. They looked at it with wonder; on guard at first, but relaxed after a few moments. It looked harmless and they slowly approached it. They saw how it was grazing on grass, so they plucked up a handful to feed to him. It took some steps back at first, but then, to their surprise, came up and began munching on it off their hands. They were utterly amazed at its majestic form and petted it, bewildered that it didn't seem frightened. They thought it must have been an animal from the Old World, not seen since from dwelling in the wilderness. They talked about, thinking of trying to name it for themselves, when Zempher caught sight and told them it was indeed a horse. He said how people used to keep and ride them, but that one wasn't broken.

As they returned on their way, they looked back to see it still gazing at them. The creature only strengthened their love for wildness and lack of fetter. Peter noticed how free it was, never knowing what the novel planet of Anathea-ism was, and never having changed because of it. It was truly a living, untarnished relic.

Ten additional miles in, they came to a break in the woods, and found themselves in a meadow. It was a mass grave of bodies half-burnt. The smell was indescribable and they were forced to cover their mouths with clothes. Seagulls flew around and picked at the corpses. It was a very bad sign. It meant that people were around and, most importantly, Guards. Yet, it also signaled that they were near the ocean and grew jovial because of it.

They obviously did not stay long.

Alas, five miles further, they heard the sound of waves crashing against rocks. They hurried their footsteps faster than ever. Indeed, soon afterwards, the forestline broke yet again, and they came out, seeing the grand sight of a long, stormy beach. Arra, Knox, and Zempher ran to the pier to quickly look around.

Meanwhile, Peter and Janet (holding Hannhia), looked at each other with elation. They both unspokenly knew that a new future awaited them. Peter put his arm around her and told her everything was going to change for the better; so long as Arra succeeded in her knowledge of the island.

The pier was completely absent of people, but Peter noticed a stray Guard almost a mile away, doing something along the sand. Immediately, Peter and Janet ran over to the others and relayed the danger. They all hid in a dilapidated boat; frantic about what to do. Still, it was more important than ever that they found a working vessel, so Peter and Knox silently and carefully went from boat to boat.

Suddenly, fifteen minutes later (which seemed like an eternity), Peter turned a corner to go outside and came face-to-face with the soldier standing in front of him. The guard slowly began to raise his weapon–not even questioning them first, inquiring why they were there–and Peter knew he'd have to act fast.

At once, Peter leapt onto him and fought him. The Guard knocked him solidly in his jaw, and Peter likewise did the same. Peter tried desperately to take his gun from him, yelling loudly for help. The Guard was far more muscular and, with another blow to Peter's face, swiftly threw Peter to the ground beside him. He tried to stand and point his gun at the boy when, out of nowhere, ringing loudly, and echoing through the dark sky, a gunshot went off.

The Guard stared at Peter for a brief second before dropping his weapon and falling on Peter. The Guard looked up to the Heavens, praying to Anathea; begging her that he lived a noble life and was prepared to die, for it was his time. He turned his head to Peter, telling him he'd never know the divine kingdom with her: that he was scum, bringing harm to one of her children. The boy, for some odd reason, felt bad for him. God only knew all of the terrible deeds he'd done and truly deserved punishment, but he'd been misguided since birth, having never heard a word that contradicted what his peers told him.

Looking up, Peter saw Knox a little ways away to the back of the soldier. He looked in shock, never having killed someone. Peter, with a bloody face, got up and took the gun from him, thanking him while they both looked at the dead man.

Knox couldn't speak. He'd beat people before, but never took their lives. Perhaps he felt like one of them–the bad guys. Inside, however, he could justify it. It was kill or be killed, and the Guard deserved death far more than his friend.

Finally, he stuttered and let out the sentence, "I found a boat".

Peter quickly ran to tell the others, not even mentioning the killing. They rushed over to Knox who snapped out of it and led them. Surely, even from two or three miles away from the flat ground, others could've heard the shot. Hopefully, they thought it simply came from their comrade, but they'd eventually see him not return, so they had no time to lose.

They entered a small fishing boat. It was old, rusted, slightly broken down, but was seaworthy and therefore perfect.

As they entered, frantic yet smiling, Knox was about to enter when he handed Knox his gun back, telling him he had to stay. They all looked at him with great confusion, yelling at him to get on and questioning why not.

Janet passed Hannhia over to Arra and ran over to Peter, pleading with him and almost in tears. He told her it was okay and that he had a duty to fulfill. He knew she'd be set free, happy, and no longer destitute. Her life mattered more than his.

She hugged him tightly, desperately attempting to convince him otherwise and telling him he was being foolish. He kissed her, explaining he needed to help save others, no matter what–that he felt it was his purpose. He wanted to relieve and release them from the wrath of Gabriel's dystopia.

She began crying and he demanded she leave, for the Guards would show up soon. Again, they kissed and Janet said she'd never forget him and always loved him deeply. She looked over and saw two other Guards about a mile and a half away through the mist. She forced herself to break free of holding hands and rushed over to the others.

Knox started the engine and they all looked at Peter–as he did with them–while the vessel gently and slowly began to move forward. Knox threw him a long-distance walkie talkie so they could still keep each other updated on their happenings. They'd all miss him, but he may have felt the pain most. They were his only friends and family and he'd have no one once back in the city. It utterly destroyed his insides, knowing all the wonderful things he could have experienced with them if he only climbed the rungs of the ladder. It was then that he was certain his life no longer mattered; only his impact and he couldn't waste it.

They continued to look upon one another until finally, the boat became engulfed in the thick fog over the water and the sound of the engine, which had progressively became fainter, ceased to be heard.

After minutes went by and the boat had been long gone, he continued to stand there, not knowing why, other than wanting to look at the last place they were in and not wanting to abandon it any further. He saw the Guards coming closer in the distance and forced his feet to move.

He hurriedly entered back in the woods and ran as far as he could for the remainder of the day, not even stopping to eat nor drink, until he was pressed to rest and make camp. Again, he sat lonesomely beside the fire, imagining the others were there with him. The thought of him remaining there crossed his mind several times. He knew it was possible; a sweet thought even, to live the rest of his life there as a hermit. Still, doing so would be for naught. He left the group for the ability to help people. Were he to stay in the woods, leaving his friends would mean nothing and their separation would be in vain.

The next day, he had rushed enough on his own to make it back to the city in the late evening–just in time to attend work the following morning. He lay in his hidden crawlspace as usual, disheartened and anxious. It was then that he heard his radio go off. It was Janet speaking from the other side. She informed him that Knox said they were already close to the island and would arrive in about four or five days if everything worked out accordingly.

She said how she found his journal and letter. She was in the middle of reading and told him how beautiful it was. She's read it to Hannhia once grown and to her future children. She then talked about his letter, flattered that he'd really felt so strongly for her. She already knew that, obviously, but he'd never put it in so many good words.

Peter was both sad and happy for her. If she made it, he could die a contented man, and what happened to him thereon wouldn't matter. She excitedly told him all the things they were planning on doing. They'd start a small commune of their own, eventually forming their own town, of sorts. All were unaware of what dwelt on the island—only that there were almost certainly no Guards nor Order. Perhaps there'd already be a remote, free civilization, or remnants of ones. Buildings, homes, supplies; they could be there, whether with people or not. Fear and judgment would soon be foreign concepts to them and they'd speak and refine their skills of the Old Language and Old Ways. In time—far down the road, when a considerable amount of people populated it—they could make their own government; it'd be a Democracy. Religions could thrive, but all could choose their own, save Anathea-ism: the only one sure to bring horror and destruction.

Peter's eyes watered, yet it was overshadowed by a tranquil smile. The tears were part-sadness, part-joy. They'd speak the rest of the night until both fell softly asleep, comforted by each other's reposeful voices.

CHAPTER 16

Life and Death

Peter awoke at about 8:00 AM. He was slightly hungover from the night before and had a small headache piercing the behind of his eyes; no matter, however, the time had come and his conscience was fully recovered from the mental hardships of the day prior. He was ready to set things right, regardless if it'd be a fool's errand. He could only pray things would go as planned. In truth, though, he had little faith, and a thick veil of doubt clouded his mind. Would it truly work? Would it be effective? He could only speculate with little to go off of.

As per usual, he threw on his jumpsuit and was about to head out the door until he was stopped by the sight of a picture frame atop a drawer. It was a family photo from when he was a young boy about five. His mother and father stood by him, holding his hands, and looking happy. It warmed his heart, thinking about them. It was not an Old World photo, but he imagined it looked similar to one. They stood in a garden; one unknown its location. Gardens–at least in the slums–hadn't existed for decades. They were all dressed in rags then, as expected, but they stood as though they wore beautiful clothes; completely carefree of wheresoever they were at and what was happening around them. A strong sentiment of happiness washed over, which was confusing, knowing they were all gone. Maybe he'd soon be with them.

Peter soon arrived at the Department, walking in inconspicuously and normally. He chose to come early that day, before most of his coworkers; it was safer that way. At his desk, he paid diligent attention to the newsroom about fifty feet away. Once the cameras were on, it was go time. Watching the clock incessantly, he got up and pretended to use the restroom. In actuality, he went to the camera control room. It was generally filled with only three or four men–not the biggest hurdle. Looking both ways in the halls to ensure an absence of peeking eyes, he slowly and quietly turned the knob to the room and peered in.

He took out a handful of Knox's knockout bombs and rolled them on the ground; therewith he reached his hand around the wooden, heavy door and locked it from the inside. He waited a few minutes further until he was sure they'd fainted. Then would death surely come.

He again sat at the desk until finally, the final person, a maintenance man, left out of the newsroom. It was his chance to strike. He walked back to the hallway, pulled the fire alarm, at which time panic ensued.

Once a sufficient number of people evacuated, he leapt into the newsroom and barricaded the door with anything he could. Sheer fear fell upon him and his heart began to race. That was it, he thought. There was no turning back. His words would resonate or they would rebound and strike him. Either way, he wasn't leaving a free man.

He saw the lights on the main camera blink; a good sign, it was on and broadcasting. The bombs must've worked and the controllers were fast asleep. He stared into it for a minute, knowing that every word he'd say from then onward would mean more than all the books he'd ever read. He had only one chance and everything–changing the minds of at least a hundred, affecting the West in some manner, but more so in terms of his safety, road on it.

He first introduced himself. He explained his job and all the corrupt duties he was asked to perform: how propaganda worked and was created, how most rebellions were staged, and why his bosses couldn't have cared less about the people–only their statuses and credit.

Explanation then swiftly morphed into anger. Peter, in great desperation, earnestly proclaimed all the viewers fools; that they lived in a dystopia of their own creation and worse: they saw evil, death, punishment, oppression, as the epitome of civilization. They truly believed that the most benevolent god that was theirs, imposed a society of fear, intense persecution, unrestrained hatred and intolerance, lack of love to others, and tyranny disguised as "order". They were forbidden to worship idols yet saw Gabriel as the greatest possible human who ought to have temples and statues built in his honor. Somehow in their twisted, stretched brains that had great abilities performing mental gymnastics, they saw it as noble to cut the heads off animals, whip and kill the poor, snigger at the innocent, scold the freethinkers and individuals, and laugh and spit in the faces of those who merely misspoke.

He then brought out the old, rusty Iphone, and turned on a video of Arra in the food plants. The disgusting acts and food processed there would make any cringe, but he berated them that they thought such things were normal.

At that point, the fire alarm went off and he knew the Guards would soon run up to the floor. The news station was the largest in the whole Pacific Northwest and the broadcast reach would be seen by millions–if not hundreds of millions–of people.

He spoke to them in Old Language tongue. Perhaps they wouldn't have fully understood it, but he had to prove a point. He showed them that the language was not evil and caused no harm. They had descended so far to think that mere words equated violence. He pleaded that nothing happened; that if it was so wicked, Anathea should have smote him and caused him to fall dead right then and there. Yet, he was safe.

"Do you really wish to live in perpetual fear?" He said. "That everything you do–no matter how minuscule–is used against you?"

While on the phone, he put it in front of the camera and played a quick montage of a JFK speech. To him, the words were extraordinary and represented much of the proper ways to live and thrive.

He heard footsteps running downstairs and sped up his pace even more. He turned on a hologram of a Christmas parade while he continued.

He read off the screen excerpts of the Constitution and Bill of Rights last spoken so long ago: *We the People,…establish Justice, insure domestic Tranquility, provide for the common defense, promote the general Welfare, and secure the Blessings of Liberty to ourselves and our Posterity, do ordain and establish this Constitution for the United States of America.*

The country shall make no law respecting an establishment of religion, or prohibiting the free exercise thereof; or abridging the freedom of speech, or of the press; or the right of the people peaceably to assemble, and to petition the Government for a redress of grievances.

"Does that sound unreasonable?" He pleaded. "It was not Anarchy as our leader says. Our world was once ruled by the people; each and every one of us. You honor and praise a god that created you to be slaves. She is vengeful and wrathful and bloodthirsty, yet you believe her to be all-merciful and the bearer of light at the same time? She contradicts herself and your faith lies with one man alone: he who desires to control every inch of your bodies and movements. He subdues you and forces pleasure with drugs so you're blinded from the bleakness, starkness, and misery that lies around every corner. Even now, you doubt a man speaking sincerely, who cares for freedom and your prosperity to live as you chose, faithful in love and autonomy! Don't worship me, give consideration to the notion of independence and a planet without hellish pressure."

Suddenly, there was banging and shouting at the door. He did the only thing he could; his last resort to spare his life.

He lied and proclaimed to have raised an army of 20,000 rebels–truly freedom fighters for their honest welfare. He said how they were close by, hidden in an unknown location that only he himself knew of, until Peter gave the command. They'd storm the dictator's castle and assassinate him.

The banging intensified.

"If he's truly the chosen one," he said, "watch if his goddess saves him. Join us and raise your pickaxes. Battle not a religious war, but one for the sake of choice and liberty."

He continued his last-ditch, desperate oration for minutes afterwards until finally, a swat team of Guards burst down the make-shift barricade. They lined up and pointed their rifles straight at his eyes, when Peter's boss stepped through them and said, "Not yet. *He* wants to see him. He can be made an example out of."

They hurried over to Peter and hit him hard across the face, while others kicked and punched his body. As he soon fainted, a Guard injected him with a substance and he fell deeply asleep.

The following day, a rebellion did indeed take place. Unfortunately, it was only a group of a hundred people. One-hundred, in the whole world who walked without fear. They were instantly disposed of and burned in the streets. Peter's words seemed not to have affected as many as expected.

Peter awoke in a chair with his feet and arms strapped to it tightly. He looked around and saw that he was in an extremely large, elegant room with Guards lining the walls, staring at him with disgusted faces. The faint sight of a man stood about two-hundred feet in front of him. His eyes remained blurry and he was unable to make out the identity. As he walked towards Peter, he heard his voice and instantly knew who he was.

"Hello Peter." He said. "I had heard you were quite good in the propaganda sector. Unfortunate that you were such a waste."

As Peter's eyes cleared, he saw that it was him; the great man, Gabriel.

Chills went down the boy's spine. The dictator could do whatever he wished with him. Perhaps he'd be tortured: burned at the stake, filleted, fried, pierced a thousand times before the relief of death.

"I thought you'd be a valuable asset." He said. "Even for a young man, you performed better than most."

"What do you want?" Said Peter.

"I want to teach you a lesson." Gabriel responded. "You riled up quite a stir. Millions saw you and I'm sure you feel proud. Yet, do you think you accomplished anything?"

Peter simply looked with an angry, beaten face, and told him someone needed to do it–to tell the truth.

"Truth!" Said Gabriel. "And you think you know the truth? Do you know who I am? How I got to where I am?"

"I know Anathea is folly, a made-up being; and you, a fake, evil individual less than human."

"Suppose you're right, Peter, and Anathea does not exist. Isn't it fascinating that the whole world is at my command and worship her, simply by me telling them she's real with no proof? Is it not amazing how easy it is to fool people and make them compliant sheep?"

"You take advantage of their desperation." Replied Peter.

"That's where you're wrong, kid. I gave them hope. What have you done? You wished to crush their hope with Old World ideas. You want to annihilate a goddess and man who fulfills all of their inner desires. They know no concept of freedom, save that I bring them hope: a far more powerful idea than your silly *liberty* of the past. Interesting, that freedom of speech is what let me become who I am. If I let them speak as they wish now, they'd bring themselves to ruin in a day with their disagreements."

It was notable that he was speaking the Old Language; not his imaginary one that he used when making speeches. It was obvious he was the same man he was fifty years ago and didn't buy into his own preachings.

"I brought unity when there was only division." Said Gabriel. "Perhaps you see it as darkness, but not the people. The people are one; they're unified, consolidated, federated. Humans are not saints; they're not angels. They hunger for peace and for order. Can you possibly imagine a more orderly society? It's peoples' inherent nature to be selfish, autonomous, and egocentric. It has been that way since the dawn of man. Selfishness is what brings security and personal prosperity–it's why Capitalism and currency was so successful. But, they still need to be kept in check. Has there ever, in the whole of history, been a citizenry without a leader or guidance. Never. I simply created an idea and they fell at my feet, kissing them for where I walked they wished to follow. The most famous leaders were those who held iron rods and metaphorical whips; they built the grandest, most widespread empires: the likes of Genghis Khan and Stalin."

"Why was religion the most successful concept of all time?" He continued. "People need to believe someone, somewhere, looks after them, cares for them, and saves them from the toil that persists on the doleful ground we call Earth. I created the greatest hope possible and none has turned their cheek to it. I can decapitate a thousand people in an hour and people will still believe I am doing the right thing. That's how ignorant and sheepish they are. They will adhere to any idea and, the best one, is universal faith in a common goal. For the sake of them not destroying themselves, I must enforce law; without such, the planet burns overnight."

"You pretend that humans are mere simpletons–animals or scorpions. I have faith in people: that they can be good and everyone desires happiness. You spy on every inch of their lives and destroy their own beings of living as individuals. You prevent them from existing as people" Replied Peter.

"Then you're the dunce." Said Gabriel. "Tell me, would you leave a baby unsupervised? Would you trust that they can walk on their own, go to work, nurture themselves, or progress society in any way? They're all children and need my sustenance to even get along or survive. I've trained them, quite well in fact, but if I had not intervened so long ago, none of us would be here. And yet, it is ironic, that you are but a young man, but have an older soul than all of them.

Still, you shouldn't possibly hope that I will just set you free. You brought discord–regardless if you succeeded."

"Then what will you do with me?" Peter asked. "What do you hope to accomplish with me further? I knew the consequences, what they needed to hear, and I changed something in your Order–no matter how small. I am not one of them and I see through your deception. When I die, I'll perish honorably, and you, a murderer."

Gabriel simply laughed and said he'd never understand.

Peter then began to cuss at him with Old Language and insult the dictator. He said how evil he was and wouldn't go to any heaven. Gabriel, with a smile on his face, simply rebutted, "Take him now."

Again, a Guard came up to him and injected him with the same fluid that made him pass out before. Peter's eyes dropped and his vision became blurry and black and white as he watched Gabriel turn and walk back inside the castle. He could only guess what would become of him before falling out of consciousness.

Peter suddenly awoke upon a large stage outside in an unknown city. He rested on his knees, facing a massive crowd of tens of thousands of people screaming at him. He looked behind him and saw fifty guards with flamethrowers pointed their weapons at him, commanding that he not move.

To the right of him was Gabriel beside a microphone. He raised his arms up as though he was Jesus when on the cross. He yelled, "Dissent! Dissent! The time of damnation has come!" He walked towards Peter and struck him violently with a small whip across his face. The burning sensation was excruciating and his cheeks and eyes felt numb as blood rushed down.

Peter looked at the sky; it was evening time and dark gray with stormy overcast. Then his face turned to the crowd with his trembling bones. They were disgusting. Their faces were tarry;

their hair was dirty and wild; maggots flowed from the smiley, angry mouths; their eyes were black, empty sockets whence worms protruded; and their hearts beat so fast that their whole body pulsated. They raised up fists that were but emaciated bones with sharp claws, as they screeched as banshees.

Some of the Aristocrats then walked up along with Peter's main boss who shouted and denounced him as a traitor and terrorist.

"All lies!" He announced. "The words were utter lies intended to harm you! To spread heresy and lead you astray!"

Again, Gabriel threw his whip upon him; this time across the back.

It was then that a World Guard stepped forth and handed the leader the drawing found in Peter's pocket. Gabriel's visage looked furious. He opened it, held it up in front of the crowd, shouting how evil it was.

"This is his ideal life!--The Old Ways of their dystopia. He emulates it and seeks it to be our sphere. Where is Anathea in it? Where is religion? Where is the beautiful, bonafide structure that is the foundation of our New World? Witchcraft, we say!"

Gabriel then paused for a moment in silence, looking at the boy and back at the congregation. He told the size of the revolt; just how small it was, and that they'd all be saved for their faith in their goddess–for not forsaking her and the chosen one.

"She protected us from the riot, from the devilish, oppressive terrorists who seek to undermine our piety. See here this boy: how he feeds off of rotten flesh: he gains nourishment from contempt and hatred towards us."

Gabriel then slowly walked towards Peter; still with his arms raised, but this time with a dagger in his right hand. He held it tightly against Peter's throat, just enough for a thin line of blood to appear.

Naturally, Peter shouted out in supplication, begging for his life to be spared. And yet, despite the dire situation, he did not apologize. He did not bow down before the *chosen one* and beg for forgiveness of his *errors*. He knew, and always would, that he was right–that he was the true *right-human* who understood the meaning of life. Love, freedom, emancipation, and compassion–those were his principles and he was ready to die for their sake.

"Look here, behold! See his fear; his detest for death. He knows we are more powerful than him and have the authority to rip his soul from his figure. Why fear, unless one's aware of their own damnation? He knows Hell awaits him and therefore longs to live. Shall we spare him?"

The people then shouted so loud it hurt Peter's ears. They laughed, knowing Gabriel would do the correct action. They well knew the boy's time was up.

A handful of Guards then stepped up with sacks in their hands and tossed drugs out to the people.

"Be elated while we vanquish the wicked." Said Gabriel, meanwhile.

It was then that Peter saw everything in slow-motion, as one would find in a movie. He looked around, seeing all their crazed faces, staring at him violently and wishing him a horrible death. They were utter savages–thirsting for gore, yearning for pain.

Then Peter closed his eyes for a moment. He pictured Janet and his friends in his mind, how much he loved them and hoped for their safety. They were pearls lying hidden in a farm full of swine. What would they think if they knew about his situation? Surely, it'd destroy Janet. He was content knowing they were ignorant. He then didn't feel so much distress. He pictured them having arrived and living happily for years to come, even if it meant him not joining them. But, the beautiful, hopeful imagery ceased as quickly as it came.

He opened his eyes and the scene changed. The once dark, cloudy sky was a gloomy, bloody red one. The people were no longer ugly and nausea-inducing, but vile looking. They had fur on every part of their bodies, but especially their faces. They had something like small goat horns atop their heads and their eyes were glowing red. Interestingly, the children about them were an exception. The younglings, yet grown to believe in their sinister ways, looked completely normal, clueless, and innocent. Their faces were shining, blemishless, and their clothes were not rages, but sweet garments.

In a matter of only a minute, Peter, with racing thoughts, took time to think. He accepted that nothing he said nor did, regardless in its reach or multitude, could possibly matter; the people were too gone and unsaveable. He could shoot Gabriel right then and there and yet, the people would still find a way to justify his downfall. They'd declare Peter as some form of Anti-Christ and Gabriel would return in a second-coming to bring about an even greater "utopia". His desperate speech meant nothing, but there were no words to relinquish them of the tyranny. Somehow, in some way, their faith had grown so high that the threat of the most heinous form of torture would not be nearly enough to dissuade their thoughts, or give admittance that they did not believe in their made-up religion. It was like persuading a man that he could live without food or breathe water. When one is born into such a strict ideology, there is no saving them. No amount of time can change a personality, and that is well known. Mindsets, yes; but the deepest parts of personality–no. The children had yet a chance–lamentful that they'd succumb to indoctrination as everyone else. At a certain level, when hysteria becomes so affluent, it becomes commonplace and accepted as basic truth.

Indeed, truth–whether forgotten, ignored, hated, rejected, or willingly altered–will always remain immutable and invincible: an objective, perhaps most powerful, facet of existence, in which humans need not define, for it is out of the realm of interpretation. Anathea-ists altered, and likewise interpreted truth, and a pit of nefarious dogma swallowed them up because of it. Humorous, that they bathed and enjoyed in it.

They all became monsters, but not necessarily intentionally. That is not to say they were forced to become ones; no, almost all willingly followed evil from the start, but many became lost causes merely from when they were able to walk. But, it was because of what they were born into. Blame ought to fall on those who started (or rather, propagated) it all–those who pushed Gabriel's ideas in the beginning, became activists towards them, and brought the hammer down on those who opposed. The poor children knew none else than Anathea-ism; but, like their parents, they turned into the latter, even if their original hearts would never have followed it. They were a product of the times and became the dictator's own product.

Gabriel feasted off of people's vulnerabilities. He frolicked in their distress, pessimism, and despair; making good use of their exposed fear they felt in the 2020s. The people were demons, but he: satan and the puppeteer that manifested them, taking away their humanity and leaving only shells of their former selves that suckled objective sin.

And yet still, Peter prayed for them. Perhaps he did to some unknown god he wasn't aware of, or for humanity's sake. He knew inside that goodness existed in man, no matter how buried it was. People of all places had the potential to do the greatest things and succeed in their most lofty endeavors. He didn't know nearly enough of the past, only magnificent things were done. People went to the moon, people had power over their livelihood, people gave charity.

Then the dictator's last words were spoken as he looked at Peter.

"Let it be done!"

Peter looked down, thinking of Janet with a chest beating a million miles an hour. He had a flashback to a scene he was presented while taking LSD long ago. He imagined Janet and him walking in a meadow and she had a flower in her hair. They were madly in love and felt no sense of dread in the slightest. He wondered whether Heaven would be like that; not Anathea's, but some other unknown one. He lightly smiles at the thought of it.

Then, a Guard stepped up behind him. In an instant, the click of a trigger of a flamethrower was heard before all went black.

It just so happened to be at the same time that Janet stood on the beach, watching the sunset and holding Hannhia tightly. She looked onwards at the sea, smiling while a breeze brushed across her hair. She could never know the fate of Peter, only admiring him that he did the right thing, whether or not his plan worked. She then looked down at the baby while soft tears ran down her face. She wished he was there to help her raise the tender child and they could live forever. Yet, she could never dream of anything more than that they were where they stood. Finally, they were safe, they were free.

She heard the sound of Knox asking her to come help him with something. Again, she looked up towards the horizon, for the first time feeling hopeful. They'd live unchained, unbound–nevermore to experience the horrors of Anathea.